M A G A Z I N E

He also affirmed that of the various pleasures offered by literature,
the greatest is invention.

— *Jorge Luis Borges*

VOLUME 1 • NUMBER 1

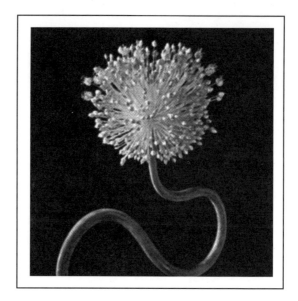

ZEFIRO

RESTAURANT + BAR

PORTLAND OREGON
500 NW 21ST AVENUE
503.226.3394

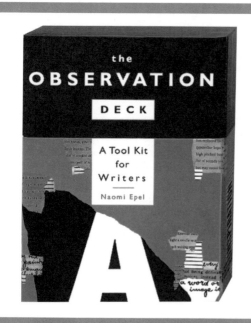

Dinh Q. Lê, *Angkor's Monkey King*, 1996, c-print & linen tape, 40" x 30"

Elizabeth Leach

GALLERY

207 Southwest Pine Street · Portland, Oregon 97204

PHONE 503-224-0521 · FAX 503-224-0844 · EMAIL eleachg@aol.com

PUBLISHER'S NOTE

"Just what the world needs—another literary magazine!" more than one of my friends has said to me sardonically, aware that there are a few hundred of the species out there on various shelves, most of them little read. Do we really need another deadly serious, under-designed, elitist publication?

In place of these customary literary quarterly sins, I wanted to create a literary magazine for the many passionate readers who are not necessarily literary academics or publishing professionals. I wanted to offer a fresh design that is elegant, readable and inviting; I wanted to include not only the best contemporary prose and poetry, but, like the most creative commercial magazines, features that would range from the challenging to the light-hearted. With this combination of ingredients, I was certain we could establish a literary magazine that is accessible to the public as well as intellectually accomplished. But there is another, over-arching reason for the creation of *Tin House*.

When I was a young student in the sixties, the watchword in academic and literary circles was that literature was dead: with the developing preeminence of television and film, the public was no longer interested in reading; after Joyce and Proust, Yeats and Eliot, there was no further place for literature to go anyway.

Well, this turns out not to be the case. The signs suggest that people are reading as much as or more than ever. There is a new and international generation of writers that has broken out of the confines of modernist exhaustion and struck out in various directions, some experimental, some quite straightforward and old-fashioned. With *Tin House*, I have set out to capture the energy and intensity of the best new writers from around the world. For me, publishing *Tin House* is a dream fulfilled.

We urge you to join us as we begin this adventure.

Win McCormack

Win McCormack, Publisher/Editor-in-Chief

FICTION

NEW VOICES

POETRY

POETRY
[CONTINUED]

PROFILES

PILGRIMAGE

FEATURES

FEATURES
[CONTINUED]

LOST AND FOUND
IN PRAISE OF UNDERAPPRECIATED BOOKS AND AUTHORS

A READABLE FEAST

THE LAST WORD

PHOTOGRAPHS BY PIPO

Editor-in-Chief/Publisher
WIN McCORMACK

. . . .

Editors
ROB SPILLMAN AND ELISSA SCHAPPELL

Managing Editor
HOLLY MacARTHUR

Senior Editor
TUCKER MALARKEY

Poetry Editor
AMY BARTLETT

Contributing Editors
AGHA SHAHID ALI • DOROTHY ALLISON • ALBERTO FUGUET
JEANNE McCULLOCH • CHRISTOPHER MERRILL • RICK MOODY
HELEN SCHULMAN • TOM SPANBAUER • IRVINE WELSH

Editorial Interns
CHRISTINA CHIU • SERENA CRAWFORD

Photo Consultant
RANDY GRAGG

Art Director
JON BAIRD

. . . .

Tin House is published quarterly by McCormack Communications. Vol. 1, No. 1, Spring 1999.
Printed by Edwards Brothers, Ann Arbor, MI. Price for single issue in USA: $10.
Send subscriptions requests or manuscript (with SASE) submissions to: P.O. Box 10500, Portland, OR 97296-0500.

EDITORS' NOTE

Welcome to our house. Let us show you around the pad.

The name *Tin House* comes from our Portland office, a Victorian house literally covered in tin, a strangely arresting landmark, a Modigliani in a neighborhood of Hoppers. *Tin House* is a similar oddity, a literary magazine with a mission to be readable, even interesting. We're a bi-coastal, international magazine with contributing editors scattered from San Francisco to Santiago, from Edinburgh to New York. *Tin House* is a haven for writers and readers who are unconcerned with the latest or the trendiest, a safe house for the most provocative and engaging writing.

Along with poetry and fiction, look for regular columns on food and drink, pilgrimages to the sacred and profane, profiles and interviews with literary and non-literary heroes, satire, and a section for writers to champion their favorite underappreciated authors and out-of-print books, as well as portfolios from visionary photographers and artists.

Our staff and contributors are geographically scattered, varied in our interests, but united by the conviction that good writing can change your life, that authentic writing is still the purest form of intellectual engagement.

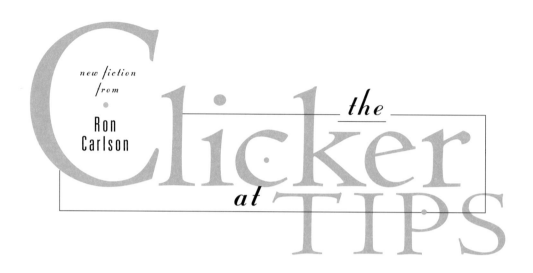

new fiction from

Ron Carlson

the Clicker at TIPS

BY THE TIME I PULLED OPEN THE BIG WOODEN DOOR
OF TIPS, EVE HAD FINISHED OFF A THIRD OF THE ENGLISH
BEER MENU. SHE WAS SITTING DEAD CENTER IN THE
MIDDLE OF THE BIG EMPTY BARROOM LIKE A LOST CHILD.

On the other side of the bar station two guys played pool at one of the twelve tables. The floor in Tips was varnished cement; it was not a very comfortable place, but they filled it every night with all the young brokers who were still in mourning for college.

"Did you notice how there's no work anymore?" she said when I sat down.

"This place used to be a factory."

"I work," I said.

"No you don't. You fly around and talk for money."

"Eve," I said. "You don't think air travel is work?"

"You get introduced, walk to the podium, always a nicer piece of furniture than I have in my whole house, and then you pause a beat because you're sure that every eye is on you, then you pause again and then you give your lecture. Afterward they hand you a big check. They pay you for those pauses."

There was an edge in it, I could hear it, but Eve always had an edge. I had wanted to see her; it had been two months, silence since our last meeting, dinner downtown. I was surprised that her mention of her house, the rooms of which I knew well, had quickened everything.

The waitress came over, a tall young woman with long braids. "Did one of you guys want the clicker?"

"Moi," Eve said, presenting her palm. The girl placed the television remote control in it. The five televisions around the room were all set on the pregame show. I asked the waitress for a pint of Bass.

"Are we on television?" I asked Eve.

"We are. We're on the six-fifteen."

"Who are you scolding today?"

"That same sleazeball with the jewelry."

"What did he say?"

"He was able to push me down and stride nobly to his Lexus. That's why I want to see it." Eve was ombudsman for channel 14, sniffing out consumer complaints. Last week she'd put a bottled-water company out of business and this week it was this guy, Gene Somebody, and

his fake Navajo jewelry.

"Are you all right?"

"I'm fine. I sat on my ass in Scottsdale and did the report and realized I hadn't been pushed to the ground since you took that privilege two years ago."

"Eve," I said.

"Let's have another pint." She was speaking over my head to the waitress, who came round and set my beer smoothly on the table. "But something from the Continent now. Something from some country that doesn't even exist anymore."

"Pardon?" the waitress said.

"Eve wants the Yugoslavian lager," I told her. I looked at my full glass. "Make it two."

"Yes, the little hero comes to the door, sees the mike, and bolts. Some sixty-year-old in tight jeans pushes me down. I just want to see it. Is this a soulless place or is it me?" She drank and looked at me. "God, what a word and me to use it."

"It will have soul in a thousand years."

"Should we wait? Pardon: should I wait?" She pointed the remote at the television near us and it flipped forward to 14 where our pal Jeff Nederhaller was anchoring the news with Monica Young. Jeff had been part of our pretty tight circle a few years before; we had all worked at the newspaper.

I said, "Jeff looks good. Everyone should get divorced."

"He's nuts. He is an outright idiot. Marriage keeps people fat and sane."

"Very fine. So I'm sane."

Eve drilled me with a look. "Oh, are you married?"

"Eve," I said. "Let's have a nice time. Let's have a few beers and a nice time."

Around us the place was filling with the Monday night football crowd, clusters of six and eight people pushing tables together, hanging their coats on the backs of the heavy wooden school chairs, ordering

at me and said, "Oh don't be so smug. Take your jacket off, let's see your stripes."

I did, hanging my tweed coat on the chair. She scanned my black polo shirt and said, "You dress like an actor."

I considered commenting on her sleek silk dress, dark green, the black sash around her waist, how she looked good, dressed not to kill but certainly to harm, and in the half second I had that thought it settled on me how good she looked, not the dress but the choice of it. She was beautiful, smart; she looked in every way superior. She was impeccable, always. No wonder the scared little guy pushed

> 'Marriage keeps people fat and sane.'
> 'Very fine. So I'm sane.'
> Eve drilled me with a look. 'Oh, are you married?'

pitchers of imported beer.

The group beside us watching the corner TV all wore blue blazers and pinstriped shirts, a kind of uniform, young guys with great hair, talking loudly and making bets on the Bears. Some of them were from Chicago. There were days when everyone in Phoenix seemed to be from Chicago.

"Laborers," Eve said. "Stevedores."

"Middle management from Motorola," I said.

"Longshoremen, teamsters." She looked

her down. "You're dressed like a guy whose latest movie we should have clips of, someone who flew in from the coast. The whole world's a talk show."

"That it is."

"So, Matt, what's your latest project?" She wanted me to start being clever, to fence, to fight.

"You called, I came along."

"Such power." She drank her beer and narrowed her eyes. "Out of affection or fear?" The room was picking up, voices through the muffled waves of clicking pool balls.

"Eve, you're wearing me out." I toasted her. "I was thirsty."

After a car commercial, there she was on the screen in that green dress holding a microphone in front of her face. She looked smart and serious, and when she pointed behind her to the storefront, Anasazi Gems, in the sunny little strip mall, and turned, the camera followed her. The man in jeans had just emerged and was locking the glass door when Eve stepped back in frame, poised if not smug, and said, "Mr. Fuller, Eve Moran from Channel Fourteen News. We've had your genuine Indian jewelry analyzed by two independent experts and they're telling us that it's imported. Could you tell—" This was when we saw the sky for a moment as the camera was jarred, and then there was a tilted shot of Mr. Fuller boarding his silver Lexus and then an unsteady pan back to Eve sitting in the gravel of the little parking island. She didn't miss a beat. She didn't even try to get up, but turned her legs to one side as if she were sitting on the deck of a yacht and went on. "We tried to contact Mr. Fuller's workshop in Payson but the phone was disconnected some time ago and the address we received is that of the Sunshine Laundry and Dry Cleaners, which has been at their location for more than twenty years." Sitting like that, holding the mike up, her knees to one side, Eve looked beautiful. "In Scottsdale, this is Eve Moran, Ombudsman, Channel Fourteen News."

The screen went back to the console two-shot of Jeff Nederhaller and Monica Young and they said something, a joke about the news being a rough business, and thanked Eve for that report.

"Fabulous," I said, meaning it. "And you're okay?"

"I took Chuck for margaritas at a little place two doors down, a dive. He got a black eye from that bump on the camera."

"Chuck's a good guy," I said. "This is two lawsuits and a written apology."

"Please. It's a black eye, a sore ass, and the afternoon off." She smiled. "Though I do think that was a stunning report. Did you see that gravel?"

"You're something else."

"Again, please. Save that for someone you're willing to seduce." She looked at me over her glass. "Although I'm glad to hear you still love me. How's Debbie?"

"How's Debbie?" I said the name and felt it ring the way your wife's name rings in such places at such times. "Debbie is fine," I said. "She's working with the utility commission. Debbie's fine. She's having a success actually."

"We never thought anything but success for that girl." I could hear the faint echo of those margaritas in Eve's voice.

The game had come on all over the bar except for our television, which was now on *Hard Copy*. In the corner near us the group of young regulars had now circled their chairs around two of the little tables and were making noises about Chicago this, Phoenix that, even though it was going to be a one-sided exhibition. There were five or six guys; they leaned back in their chairs and pointed at the screen from time to time, yucking it up. They got to me for all the wrong reasons. I didn't envy them so much as want to correct them, ask them to display some real camaraderie, some real something the way I had with my friends Eve and David and Christopher and Jeff and Deborah, now Debbie, my wife, how we had met and hung out in the real places like a kind of family over an evening of drinks and appetizers, plate after plate, and the way we had talked wickedly, tenderly, and we all knew that those hours once or twice a week were our real lives, the center. One thing led to another; there was a sense of things happening. I hated these young guys and their surface lives, a night with the football

game. I hated the evening coming on this way, and my life, one good part of it, over.

"You're looking anemic," Eve said. "Sorry you came? I haven't seen you in, what? Two months."

"I'm fine," I said, finishing my second beer. I signaled the waitress and she stopped. "Let's have some Red Stripe," I told her.

"And a little tequila?" Eve said. "You always like a shot with your Red Stripe."

Her remembering tapped me a little, but I didn't miss a beat. "Right then," I said. "Shots." The young woman and her braids went off. "What do you hear from Christopher?"

"Christopher has not called me," Eve said. "My sources tell me he's become a naked careerist at the paper, kissing editorial butt long into the night."

Christopher had taken the features job at the paper and had his little photograph above the keystone column twice a week. When he first got on, Eve used to clip the picture and affix it to envelopes like a stamp and drop them by the various offices with a phony cancellation.

"He doesn't need to do that; he's the best writer they've got. If we'd stayed we might have learned to write."

"A dripping success like the rest." Eve lifted the remote and began leafing through the channels.

"Are they going to show your assault again at ten?" I asked her.

"I'm afraid it's the only news they've got, unless there's been a solution in Bosnia." She stopped at a black-and-white screen: the ocean, a frigate in a gray studio gale. Errol Flynn was in trouble on the high seas. "Jesus," Eve said. "Look. A real movie about real work."

"I'm not sure."

"It's a real ship in real jeopardy, storm-tossed. Every man on that vessel is thinking about his god."

"That vessel is five feet long being tossed by a wave machine in a studio pool."

The waitress came and set our drinks on the table; there was now a city of glasses. I touched Eve's glass and tossed mine back and she matched me, biting on the lime in the wake.

On the screen a man climbed in the rigging. Eve was getting loud: "The man holds a knife in his teeth while he risks death high above the deck." Eve was loud; several heads turned. "His fucking knife in his teeth."

I'd seen this; she wouldn't stop until there was trouble. She'd get loud and end up crying and I'd hold her until she was certain I was miserable, my shirtfront wet, wrecked from her crying; we'd get in her car and there would be some kissing until she was absolutely certain that I was more miserable than she was, and then she'd get straight, sit up, be brave, and we'd part, promising to call. It was a friendship; it was that thing, the post-coital friendship, always hard to balance. We'd been lovers for three months two years ago. I had been in the process of getting married at the time, and it all had been a dangerous game, I mean Eve knew I wasn't going to marry her. She came to the wedding and glowed there, wearing the occasion on her chest like a medal. I've known her for a long time and she never stood as tall as she did that day, her chin a lesson for the congregation, an inside joke for our office friends. She immediately started going with Christopher, also a joke, two careerists, doomed from the get-go. Now we did this, she called, we met, I took my medicine. The drinks had registered in me a little, but I was pretty sure I wanted it over now.

Errol Flynn was back on deck, his face wet, hurrying to organize the men on the ship, and I reached across Eve and took the remote and changed the channels until Arvell Larsen, the weather guy, popped up. She turned her head with great care toward me and said, "I wasn't going to make a scene. I was just happy to finally see a man with a knife in his mouth climbing the rigging. It's been a while." She lifted her glass and it seemed to light her; her clear handsome face was compelling. She had a kind of hard perfection that was wonderful on television. People who just met her always looked twice in the first minute. "Can you stay? We could order some food. You like the quesadilla, right?"

I looked at her. I like to look at people, I like the charged moments and Eve knew it, accused me of being addicted to them and thereby manipulative, coy, fake, an asshole. We had eye contact there, and anybody can say what they want to say, but eye contact is it, the beginning, middle, and end. It is better and worse, stronger than fondling in a hallway, stealing a kiss, better than any touch, and I held the look, feeling it work in me, glide, and then I reset myself and opened my mouth.

"You better not," she said. "Not that our gal Debbie has assumed an interest in cooking or learned to cook or even how to gather and prepare half a meal, but it will be dinnertime soon, and where is the husband? Shall we picture her there in your bright new kitchen, standing at the ready as if to open the fridge: what is that worried look on her face? I'm being such a bitch here. Is she concerned about her mate or. . . . fuck it, Matt. This is just the way I talk. I like Debbie. You can't stay to eat. And me, what do I want to do, eat bar food with some man? Please, forget I said anything."

Our table already looked like the party was over, seven glasses, two bottles, two napkins, assorted silverware splayed

Eye contact is it, the

around the ashtray, the plastic bib holding the drink specials on one side and the appetizers on the other. I began to line up the silverware. It had been an old game of ours to remove the card with the appetizer specials on it, fold it inside out, and write notes, sayings, mine always being, "A thirsty man has nothing for tears." Now, I just lined it up with the rest of the gear; I was lining things up. The late sun had dropped to the roadway and shot three powerhouse beams through the room, making the whole place only brown and gold, a science fiction scene, too bright, dangerous, throwing the shadows of the pool players against the far wall like storm clouds for a beat, and then a moment later, as I finished my pathetic organizing of our tabletop, it all broke, the square girders of light dissipating into the bogus brown bar light, and we both looked up at our television for a moment, a woman identical to Eve with a microphone in front of an apartment building in New York. We couldn't hear what she was saying.

I took a drink of the Red Stripe. "I like the bottles as much as the beer," I said.

beginning, middle, and end.

It is better and worse, stronger than fondling in a hallway, stealing a kiss, better than any touch.

Eve leveled her look at me. "That's the way it is."

"The worst beer bottle?" I asked.

"Michelob," she said without hesitating. "Stupid. Designed for nothing. Looks like it should be full of children's shampoo."

I smiled. "You're sharp," I said.

"Don't you patronize me," Eve said, pointing the television remote at my chest, "You can leave anytime you want, but do not sit there and try to kiss my ass."

There was a cheer from the corner and the tall guy in a blue pin-striped shirt stood and raised his arms in a victory salute. Eve went on, "But this isn't a good idea, is it? Idle chatter. We were smart and good at it once but it was because it led somewhere. We'd meet and fence and once you saw how bright I was again we'd go to bed. No, it is what it is: idle chatter." We watched the tall guy high-five his buddies, and Eve pointed. "There you are now. You had a couple like that; it's a good shirt for you, so blue, so noncommittal."

Now I was ready to get out. The beer was good and I always liked the rush of being with Eve, being seen with her, but I wanted to leave, get back to my life. Eve pointed the remote at the tall young man, and I saw the channel change over there.

"Oh my god," Eve whispered.

"What did you do?" I asked her.

There was an uproar from his mates, one cried out, "What'd you do, Ted!" and Ted turned and opened his arms before them, *I'll take care of this*, and reached up to the elevated screen and put it back on the game. He turned and pointed at the guy who had complained, said something, and they all laughed.

"When you'd come to work in those shirts, I couldn't wait for you to take your jacket off, come by my desk." Eve wasn't looking at me. "They have a nice upper yoke, well made, and the cotton is satisfying to iron. The first time I saw that shirt, I knew you'd put it on the back of the rocker in my bedroom."

"I remember that chair."

"Don't remember it," she said. Again she touched the remote and we heard the group in the corner complain. Ted stood and reached up for the controls. He looked at something standing there in the corner of the dark brown room. Eve let him right the set and sit down before she did it again. Now several loud curses sounded, and Ted, of course, stood and tried to fix the problem. "Don't remember my furniture." The channels in the corner were spinning in a blur. "My furniture is not your concern, thank you, mister."

There was, for one moment, a tumult in the corner, one guy yelling out "What!" and also standing. "This is not a good idea!" he called to the room in general.

Eve looked at me. There were no tears there, and no gloating. "You think things happen and then they get to be good ideas later? Is that what we did? Dive in and then hope it was something even workable?" She stopped their television at a car commercial, some sleek vehicle on a winding wet country lane, an unreal place.

I told her the truth: "I wouldn't know an idea, Eve, let alone a good one. I wanted to sleep with you, anyone in this room would. Face it, you're a prize. You don't get to win. You get to be the prize." I touched her face, the skin there, knowing I could, that we were both there for this little touch.

She stood up. It was an amazing thing, her standing next to me, so beautiful, her body in a green dress, her posture impeccable in the lost light. She pointed the remote at the television now and held it like the beam that held the entire room hostage, and I felt it that tight, like some cord that when it snapped would rock us all, and so I simply sat and let all my stupidity gather. Behind me in the big space, the pool balls nickered.

The young man Ted looked over at us, turned, a handsome figure in the dim light. He moved toward us with a kind of bounce in his step, a young guy in a pin-striped shirt, and he was angry, the look on his face was exactly *What the hell?* I'd already made up my mind if there was a fight I would fight, and I knew what I would say afterward in the short term and the long term, and I was gladdened to be wrong, sitting there so wrong, waiting for this fine young man. Where had he been? I'd been waiting to meet this guy for a long time. ▪

The Closet

NUAR ALSADIR

About to spill, the shape
of man, it opens. The soul,

in its many blouses, waits.
Gravitational or otherwordly,

I don't know which thrust makes
relative of wood. And of shoe,

a lower beauty: anima not in
whole, but right relation to foot.

TEMP := @TEXT@ROUND(13 * @RANDOM +1)); @IF(NUMBERS = "" I!@ISMEMBER(TEMP; NUMBERS); @SETFIELD("NUMBERS"; NUMBERS: TEMP), "")

RICK MOODY

A Tin House Contributing Editor's oblique strategy for appreciating Brian Eno, musician, producer, philosopher, and illusive inspiration.

My maternal grandmother was ill most of my early childhood. She died of cirrhosis when I was five. I didn't know her really. She had huge closets for her gowns and blouses and shoes and nightdresses, mirrored closets that ran on opposite walls in the corridor between her bedroom and her bath. I think the extremity of her demise, her sadness and loneliness, her alcoholism, her frequent threats of self-slaughter, were implicit in the fact of my sister and brother and I spending a lot of time in that corridor, trying to catch glimpses of the endless, regressive doubles of ourselves in those facing mirrors. The silence in a house of difficulties is often caught up and stored in mirrors. We summoned it forth, this silence, surviving to flee afterward into the warmth and light of the living room.

. . . .

There's a bell buoy in the harbor I particularly like. Haven't figured out why some days the foghorns perform their marine service even when the sky is clear. The interval between tollings of the buoy is unfixed, according to wave and tide; the interval

Brian Eno by Nick White

spontaneity of, say, Stockhausen or Brian Eno. On foggy nights, it's choral. Other days, there's just a bell buoy out there.

. . . . . .

Not Enough Africa. Eno's response to the lockstep of much sequenced electronic music of the nineties (acid house, techno, breakbeat, drum and bass). What *Africa* means in this observation, I'd argue, is polyrhythms, and the tendency in African music for rhythms and meters to come and go in a flexible way in a piece of music. Or maybe *Africa* suggests the importance of improvisation, or maybe both of these things. One tends to overlook, in Eno's music—which often feels very European, very indebted to ideas of Western music, at least in terms of melodies and harmonies—the debt to non-European sources: jazz, world music, indigenous music, sound constructions. *Not Enough Africa* is also a political perception, therefore, and as with much of what Eno has said, it is applicable to American cultural debates. Which is to say that I find myself thinking Not Enough Africa, sometimes, when listening to Strom Thurmond talk on C-SPAN. In literature this is the case, as well; wherein realism (an artificial construction, a

between the bellowings of foghorns is fixed, according to the Coast Guard; yet the precise interval is different in the case of each foghorn, so that you might locate your position, with the help of charts spread wide on the surfaces of your navigating table. All these sounds in and out of phase. Sometimes it's like the unisons of Phil Spector records, bass flute and glockenspiel and electric guitar. Then, when these signals go out of phase, it's more like the inexplicable syntactical iteration, rather than a apprehension of truth) is the dominant articulation of narrative in American fiction. *Not Enough Africa* might therefore mean not enough *myth*, not enough spontaneity in voice, too much attention to *workshop style*, too much clarity, not enough collective unconsciousness, not enough attention to the imperatives of intertextuality. On the other hand, any debate about what Africa means is essentialist, in the old-fashioned sense, because *Africa* might mean different things at different times, according to the way ideas get refracted. Essentialism itself, after all, *doesn't have enough Africa in it.*

The Dalai Lama came to meditate in Central Park. In Strawberry Fields. At Dawn. And we came up the East Side subway, from Brooklyn. Suddenly, at 4:45 A.M., the IRT was crowded with people, not *crowded* exactly, not like when you get on the number seven after a Mets game, but crowded enough with people that you weren't worried about getting rolled if you slipped in and out of consciousness, as most of us seemed to be doing, napping, and we didn't really have any idea exactly *where Strawberry Fields was*, because who pays attention to these things exactly, and

we were violating ancient parental injunctions against being *in the park at night*, or at least it looked to be night when we got off the train at Hunter College and crossed town toward the park, it was dark, and we paraded in the middle of the road, down the center of Sixty-ninth, as you get to do only during the infrequent snowstorm, unless you are the sort who still comes home from clubs at that hour, as the sun is trucked out of its warehouse in Queens. Much fog that morning in June, and we went over the wall and into the park, and we didn't know where *Strawberry Fields was*, although we knew where the band shell was, and then we heard this unearthly lowing, from some obscure quarter, and all the assembled, the faithful, the kids, the believers, the indigents, the night crawlers of the park moved through night toward this lamentation, following sound, knowing nothing more than that this sound suggested the culmination of pilgrimage. Tibet had sprung up like an alien culture in Central Park, monks on the rocks above us with their ancient wind instruments, their ceremonial horns, and so unearthly was it that all of us assumed a certain posture, unavoidably, and a black Lincoln Town Car pulled up, out climbed a distant, balding guy in an orange monk's garb, and he sat among us.

. . . .

The hydraulic brakes of New York City buses. The way dogs bark at sirens. Skips and pops and scratches on long-playing records. The answering machine messages of strangers. Save on membership *today*. The price of this admission ticket may be applied toward a new membership, if purchased today or in the next week. Dry cleaner, $9.75. Metrocard, $15.00. Taxi, $25.00. Dinner at Dok Suni's, $34.00. News, $1.10. Limit one ticket. Inquire at Lobby Membership Desk. Join now. Other Music: Black Box Recorder, *England Made Me*; Stockhausen, *Kontakte*; Ulmer, James Blood, *Harmelodic Guitar & Strings*; Throwing Muses, *In A Doghouse*; CD, *Misc Used*; Eno, Brian, *Shutov Assembly*. Retain portion for reentry.

. . . .

I toured for five or six weeks to support one of my books and I was lucky to do so, and though it was not terribly long by the standards of the Danielle Steels and Stephen Kings of the world, or by the standards of rock and roll personalities or professional sports figures, it was long for me, as I don't like to travel and am not good at small talk. By the middle of the tour I was exhausted and anxious in a way I'd rarely felt before, and I was changing planes in O'Hare, changing to a puddle jumper, which required going under the main landing strip over to the smaller terminal on the far side of the airport. *Am I certain this happened at all?* Under the strip they had a moving sidewalk, *a people mover*, a horizontal escalator, a quarter mile long, perhaps even longer, and this corridor was lit only with strange neon fixtures in the brighter tonalities. The music there, in that windowless space, was distinctly different from your standard airport diet of classics and Muzak adaptations of Motown hits. It was electronic, digital, arbitrary, ambient. It wasn't Eno's *Music for Airports*, which I bought in 1979, when it was first released, and which I have played since more or less continuously, sometimes for days at a time. It wasn't this, but it was the same idea. Without Eno's model, that corridor itself would not have existed in the way it did, nor would we have come to see airports as an opportunity for a dignified and sober space, but merely as conduits, places to be gotten through, across.

. . . .

Thursday, and the heron out in the cove is scrapping with some local gulls. Territorial, I figure. Hard to believe that a bird as beautiful as the heron (*tri-colored heron* is the only one I can find in my *Simon and Schuster Guide to Birds of the World*, though everyone here refers to them as *great blues*), could be saddled with a call as raw and unpleasant as the heron's. It's something like the righteous indignation of a season ticketholder in the thin air of the stands. I'm awake at 5:30 A.M., first light, and the heron sounds prehistoric, reptilian, so primitive is its wail during the altercation at dawn. Later in the day I go to see if I can get a look and I scare him (or her) up, off a piling on the end of a dock. The heron lifts off slowly, its reedy legs skimming the water. Then, tickling its belly on the tops of a couple of shrubs, it wheels to one side and alights on the desolate beach at the mouth of the harbor.

. . . .

I heard *Roxy Music* in 1975, when I worked at the radio station where I went to school in New Hampshire. The strange synthesizer part on "Virginia Plain" was what I loved right away, the weird noisy droning of the one-four progression that serves as a bridge in that piece. These rumblings weren't like anything else I was listening to at the time. When I figured out that these and other conceptual interludes on the Roxy album were the work of a

musician with one name only (it wasn't until later that he reverted to his full name), and that he had released records of his own, I acquired them all within a short time. By the late seventies, I would buy anything he was associated with, all of the film music, any record he produced, live collaborations (*801 Live*), fully detachable records made by musicians he used in his recordings (Brand X, Material, et al.). I was the only person I knew listening to this music. Or very close to it. Later in 1981, on a wall between Penn Station and the 34th Street subway station, I first saw that graffito of that period, *Eno is God*.

. . . .

I got to talk to him. Twenty years after first hearing his work. I was writing a piece about David Bowie for the *Times*. Eno's *people* were hard to pin down as to his whereabouts, his availability, etc. He was heading off *on holiday* and didn't want to be interrupted. Through some prodding by

Later in 1981, on a wall between Penn Station and the 34th Street subway station, I first saw that graffito of that period, Eno is God.

my editor, I was connected by telephone. I was nervous. I had spent much of my life parsing Eno's output, wondering about his next move, about the meaning of certain collaborations. Why "The Paw Paw Negro Blowtorch?" Why "King's Lead Hat?" (Because it's an anagram of "Talking Heads".) Why agree to produce the first Devo album? Because I was using the tape recorder on the fax machine in the dusty corridor of my apartment, I had to sit in there, in the hall, on the floor, with my list of questions. Perspiring. I imagined this discomfort was an influence upon Eno's answers, according to his own theory that what is of interest in a musical composition is what happens outside of the range of the microphone, the unrecordable facts of a certain production. To some of my questions, Eno was clipped and uninterested, as when I asked if he had felt any pressure to create a hit on Bowie's record *Outside* (which he produced), or when I asked if he ever read the postings about his work on the Web. On other matters, he was remarkably articulate. But as in his terrific piece for *Details*

"The point for me is not to expect perfumery to take its place in some nice, reliable, rational world order, but to expect everything else to become like perfume"

magazine on perfume ("The point for me is not to expect perfumery to take its place in some nice, reliable, rational world order, but to expect everything else to become like perfume"), Eno was always evasive *as an entity*, and later I was grateful for this, for the possibility that the meaning of Eno and Eno's output as an artist and musician was in no way consonant with Brian Eno himself, the guy on holiday who didn't want to be interrupted; the possibility existed that the process of Eno's work reflected other forces, forces that an individual called Brian Eno couldn't control or even fully describe, except perhaps laterally, as when describing perfume. Eno, then, in my encounter with him, had very little to do with Eno. I presume the same is true in the disjunction that afflicts all who are, to whatever degree, public figures. But in Eno's case, the possibility that personality and work might occasionally be confluent and occasionally not according to factors like chance—this seemed closer to his work by virtue of being, somehow, further away from it.

Once, during my high school years, during an assembly, a guy named Will gave a performance of John Cage's 4'33". He arrived in the chapel, sat down at the piano, raised the lid, and didn't play a note. We were used to recitals of Purcell or sermons about *tolerance* or *excellence*, or perhaps the school chorus would sing. This guy Will was an actor, a Thespian, an expert at the judicious prank, and so we watched him carefully, as the minutes unwound, we watched his face go through these gyrations—he was peaceful, he was fierce, he was amused—and the silence, which seemed arbitrary and accidental, began to acquire a gravity. It was the longest organized silence I'd ever experienced. You could hear a parochial controversy brewing. You could hear certain masters of Latin and math and science *wondering what the hell was going on*, while others knew, and still others knew and disapproved. It was for *our* benefit, though; it was for the benefit of the kids, and I would like to say I understood immediately, but I confess I thought it was a sham, a goof, until years later, when that silence seduced me.

Eno designed, at some point in the early seventies, a set of cards to be used as aids in creative endeavors: "These cards evolved from our separate observations of the principles underlying what we are doing." Entitled *Oblique Strategies*, some of these were very direct—*Use fewer notes*—and some really were oblique: *Go slowly all the way round the outside.* Some were very much of their time: *You are an engineer.* Some were timeless pieces of advice: *Honor thy error as a hidden intention.* The *Oblique Strategies* were never technical, as I hope these responses to Eno are not. Perhaps this is a good time to suggest that the essential works of Eno from the late seventies and early eighties were not only about process, but also about tenderness, gentleness, and attention. These qualities were at a considerable remove from most of the music I listened to during the period, which tended to be aggressive, cynical, and sloppy. But I thought then and think now that tenderness, though unfashionable, often makes for great art, for art that lasts, and that *what is neglected*, as Roland Barthes says—and the human emotions are neglected these days—often becomes the site of an affirmation. *Don't be afraid of things because they're easy to do.*

fiction

Through a rift in the mist, a moon the shade of water-stained silk. A night to begin, to begin again. Someone whistling a tune impossible to find on a piano, an elusive melody that resides, perhaps, in the spaces between the keys where there once seemed to be only silence. He wants to tell her a story without telling a story. One in which the silence between words is necessary in order to make audible the faint whistle of her breath as he enters her.

Or rather than a sound, or even the absence of sound, the story might at first be no more than a scent: a measure of the time spent folded in a cedar drawer that's detectable on a silk camisole.

For illumination, other than the moonlight (now momentarily clouded), it's lit by the flicker of an almond candle against a bureau mirror that imprisons light as a jewel does a flame.

The amber pendant she wears tonight, for instance, a gem that he's begun to suspect has not yet fossilized into form. It's still flowing undiscernibly like a bead of clover honey between the cleft of her breasts. Each night it changes shape—one night an ellipse, on another a tear, or a globe, lunette or gibbous, as if it moves through phases like an amber moon. Each morning it has captured something new—moss, lichen, pine needles. On one morning he notices a wasp, no doubt extinct, from the time before the invention of language, preserved in such perfect detail that it looks dangerous, still able to sting. On another morning the faint hum of a trapped bee, and on another, there's a glint of prehistoric sun along a captured mayfly's wings. Where she grazes down his body and her honey-colored hair and the dangling pendant brush across his skin, he can feel the warmth of sunlight trapped in amber. Or is that simply body heat?

The story could have begun with the faint hum of a bee. Is something so arbitrary as a beginning even required? He wants to tell her a story without a beginning; no, rather a story that is a succession of beginnings, a story that goes through phases like a moon, the telling of which requires the proper spacing of a night sky between each phase.

Imagine the words strung out across the darkness, and the silent spaces between them as the emptiness that binds a snowfall together, or turns a hundred starlings rising from a wire into a single flock, or countless stars into a constellation. A story of stars, or starlings. A story of falling snow. Of words swept up and bound like whirling leaves. Or, after the leaves have settled, a story of mist.

What chance did words have beside the distraction of her body? He wanted to go where language couldn't take him, wanted to listen to her breath break speechless from its cage of parentheses, to wordlessly travel her skin like that flush that would spread between her nape and breasts. What was that stretch of body called? He wanted a narrative that led to all the places where her body was still undiscovered, unclaimed, unnamed.

Fiction, which he'd heard defined as "the lie that tells a deeper truth," was at once too paradoxical and yet not mysterious enough. What was necessary was a simpler kind of lie, one that didn't turn back upon itself and violate the very meaning of lying. A lie without denouement, epiphany, or escape into revelation, a lie that remained elusive. The only lie he needed was the one that would permit them to keep on going as they had.

It wasn't the shock of recognition, but the shock of what had become unrecognizable that he now listened for. It wasn't a suspension of disbelief, but a suspension of common sense that loving her required.

Might unconnected details be enough, arranged and rearranged in any order? A scent of cedar released by body heat from a water-stained camisole. The grain of the hair she'd shaved from her underarms, detectable against his lips. The fading mark of a pendant impressed on her skin by the weight of his body. (If not a resinous trail left by a bead of amber along her breasts, then it's her sweat that's honey.) Another night upon which this might end—might end again—for good this time—someone out on the misty street, whistling a melody impossible to recreate. . .

I wanted to tell you a story without telling the story.

THREE POEMS
by
CHARLES SIMIC

Stand-in

Before they strapped him in a jacket

And stuffed his mouth with a rag,

He slipped into the empty church,

Climbed the high, dim-lit cross

And clasped the suffering Jesus,

All naked himself, clinging on tight,

The fucker. Thus the pious found him,

And ran out for help, leaving him

With one candle already sputtering

Beneath his swollen, homeless feet.

Bible Lesson

There's another, better world
Of divine love and benevolence,
A mere breath away
From this grubby vacant lot
With its exposed sewer pipe,
Rats hatching plots in broad daylight,
Young boys in leather jackets
Showing each other their knives,

"A necessary evil, my dear child,"
The old woman said with a sigh,
Taking another sip of her sherry.
For birds warbling back and forth
In their gold cage in the parlor,
She had a teary-eyed reverence.
Angelic—she called them
May she roast in a trash fire
The homeless warm their hands over,

While beyond the thinnest partition
The blessed ones stroll in a garden,
Their voices tuned to a whisper
As they dab their eyes
With the hems of their robes
And debate in their tactful way
The news of freight trains
Hauling men and women
Deeper into the century's darkness.

Interrogating Mr. Worm

So, this is the fool's paradise then?

The garden of metaphysical costume balls?

The thick dictionary of blank pages?

The lavender soap bubble floating off toward the infinite

From the roof of the confetti palace?

I only have faith in you, Mr. Worm.

You are bashful and yet appear unperturbed

As you go about your grim business

Underneath this hammock gilded by the setting sun

As it sways between the dark cypresses.

There's a carcass of a small animal

In the grass lush with wild flowers,

And the sound of an outdoor wedding party—

Cries and hoots as the bride spins and falls

With a white blindfold over her eyes.

TWO POEMS
by
C.K. WILLIAMS

Tender

A tall-masted white sailboat works laboriously across a wave-tossed bay;
when it tilts in the swell, a porthole reflects a dot of light that darts towards me,
skitters back to refuge in the boat, gleams out again, and timidly retreats,
like a thought that comes almost to mind but slips away into the general glare.

An inflatable tender, tethered to the stern, just skims the commotion of the wake:
within it will be oars, a miniature motor, and, tucked into a pocket, life vests.
Such reassuring redundancy: don't we desire just such an accessory, faith perhaps,
or at a certain age to be comforted, not daunted, by knowing one will really die?

To bring all that with you, by compulsion admittedly, but on such a slender leash,
and so maneuverable it is, tractable, so nearly frictionless, no need to strain;
though it might have to rush a little to keep up, you hardly know it's there:
that insouciant headlong scurry, that always ardent leaping forward into place.

The Poet

I always knew him as "Bobby the poet," though whether he ever was one or not,
someone who lives in words, making a world from their music, might be a question.

In those strange years of hippiedom and "people-power," saying you were an artist
made you one, but at least Bobby acted the way people think poets are supposed to.

He dressed plainly, but with flair, spoke little, yet listened with genuine attention,
and a kind of preoccupied, tremulous seriousness always seemed to absorb him.

Also he was quite good-looking, and mysterious, never saying where he'd come from,
nor how he lived now: I thought he might be on welfare, but you didn't ask that.

He'd been around town for a while, had dropped from sight for a few months, when,
one evening, he came up to me in the local bookstore; I could see he hadn't been well.

He looked thin, had a soiled sling tied on one arm, the beret he usually wore was gone,
and when I turned to him he edged back like a child who's afraid you might hit him.

He smiled at himself then, but without humor; his eyes were partly closed, from dope,
I guessed, then changed my mind: this seemed less arbitrary, more purposeful.

Still, he had to tilt his head back a little to keep me in focus in his field of vision:
it was disconcerting, I felt he was looking at me from a place far away in himself.

"Where've you been, Bobby?" I asked. He didn't answer at first, but when I asked again,
he whispered, "In the hospital, man; I had a breakdown . . . they took me away there."

Then he subsided into his smile, and his silence. "What happened to your arm?"
He dipped his shoulder, his sling opened, and cradled along his arm was a long knife.

"That looks dangerous," I said; "I need it," he came back with, and the sling came closed.
I was startled. Did he think someone was out to hurt him? Might he think it was me?

He never stopped looking at me; his agitation was apparent, and not reassuring.
We'd been friendly, but I didn't know him that well. "Where's your book?" I asked finally.

He'd always carried an old-fashioned bound accountant's ledger, its pages scrawled
with columns of poems: his "book," though as far as I knew no one but he ever read it.

Again no response; I remember the store was well-lit, but my image of him is shadow;
the light seemed extracted from his presence, obliterated by the mass of his anguish.

Poets try to help one another when we can: however competitive we are, and we are,
the life's so chancy, we feel so beleaguered, we need all the good will we can get.

Whether you're up from a slum or down from a carriage, how be sure you're a poet?
How know if your work has enduring worth, or any? Self-doubt is almost our definition.

Now, waiting with Bobby, I could tell he'd had enough of all that, he wanted out;
that may have explained his breakdown, but what was it he expected from me?

I was hardly the most visible poet around; I'd published little, didn't give readings,
or teach, although, come to think of it, maybe that's just what Bobby was after.

Someone once said that to make a poem, you first have to invent the poet to make it:
Bobby'd have known I'd understand how the first person he'd devised had betrayed him.

Bobby from nowhere, Bobby know-nothing, probably talentless Bobby: wasn't that me?
I'd know as well as he did how absurd it could be to take your trivial self as the case.

But if Bobby'd renounced poetry, what was my part to be? To acknowledge it for him?
Flatter him? Tell him to keep on? I might well have, but not without knowing his work.

Then it came to me that his being here meant more than all that—it was a challenge;
Bobby wanted to defy me, and whatever he'd taken into his mind I represented.

The truth is I was flattered myself, that it was me he'd chosen, but there was that knife.
Though the blade was thin, serrated, to cut bread, not tendon or bone, it still was a knife,

it could hurt you: despite myself, I felt my eyes fall to its sorry scabbard, and as I did,
I could see Bobby'd caught my concern: he seemed to come to attention, to harden.

Though he still hadn't threatened me quite—he never did—I knew now I was afraid,
and Bobby did, too: I could sense his exaltation at having so invaded my emotions;

an energy all at once emanated from him, a quaver, of satisfaction, or anticipation:
"This is my poem," he might have been saying, "are you sure yours are worth more?"

Then the moment had passed; it was as though Bobby had flinched, though he hadn't,
torn his gaze from mine, though it clung, but we both knew now nothing would happen,

we both realized Bobby's menace was a mask, that it couldn't conceal his delicacy,
the gentle sensitivity that would have been so useful if he'd been able to keep writing.

He must have felt me thinking that, too; something in him shut down, and I wondered:
Would he take this as a defeat? Whose, though? And what would a victory have been?

He turned then and without a word left, leaving me stranded there with my books
while he drifted out into the rest of his life, weighed down with his evasions, and mine.

I never found out what he came to in the end; I've always kept him as "Bobby the poet."
I only hope he didn't suffer more rue, that the Muse kept watch on her innocent stray.

LOST AND FOUND

A TRAIN OF POWDER

FRANCINE PROSE

If Rebecca West's masterpiece, *Black Lamb and Grey Falcon*, is required reading for anyone wishing to understand the Balkans, *A Train of Powder* should be given to every juror in every capital case to supplement the judge's instructions. Written between 1946 and 1954, these reportorial accounts of four controversial trials consider crime and punishment, innocence and guilt, retribution and forgiveness. As compelling as Court TV but without the frisson of voyeurism (and with the compensatory satisfactions of West's breathtakingly lucid prose style), these elegant narratives remind us of the preciousness and fragility of our right to trial by jury. The exercise of that right depends on impartiality, intelligence, empathy, respect for our fellow humans and, above all on the concept—the rule of law—that some of our politicians have lately labored so hard to degrade.

The book's centerpiece is "Greenhouse with Cyclamens," a lengthy three-part essay on the Nuremberg Trials. West was sent to Germany by *The Daily Telegraph* in time to cover the closing arguments and the sentencing of the Nazi leaders; she was encouraged by a lawyer who pointed out that, because of the prevailing shortage of newsprint at the time, most newspapers hadn't provided much coverage of the trials. The precision and clarity of West's observations animate her crisp sketches of the defendants:

> Hess was noticeable because he was so plainly mad; so plainly mad that it seemed shameful that he should be tried. His skin was ashen and he had the odd faculty, peculiar to lunatics, of falling into strained positions which no normal person could maintain for more than a few minutes, and staying fixed in contortion for hours. He had the classless air characteristic of asylum inmates; evidently his distracted personality had torn up all clues to his past.... Baldur von Schirach, the Youth Leader, startled

because he was like a woman in a way not common among men who looked like women. It was as if a neat and mousy governess sat there, not pretty, but never with a hair out of place, and always to be trusted never to intrude when there were visitors: as it might be Jane Eyre. And though one had read surprising news of Goering for years, he still surprised. He was so very soft.

West portrays Nuremberg as a "citadel of boredom" from which, in the trial's eleventh month, everyone longs to escape—everyone but the accused. To make us see the Nazis as eager to prolong the trial (just as we would be in their situation, if we could imagine being in their situation) she forges a daring, imaginative link between our humanity and that of men we consider morally sub-human. Similar leaps are made in the book's other essays: one of which concerns a lynching case and two others which provide accounts of British trials, one for murder, another for espionage. Though the structures of the essays often suggest the cagey withholdings and revelations of the murder mystery, the real source of narrative tension is their author's determination to get under the skins and into the psyches of everyone in the courtroom, from the French judges at Nuremberg to the South Carolinian jurors.

Characteristically, West seems to be looking everywhere at once, gazing past the quotidian rituals of the trials to observe the larger communities from which the participants come. But always her attention keeps tracking back to the accused.

West's obsession with the criminal psyche is partly metaphysical, for she is one of those writers who believe that concrete details can be piled up like a ladder to bring us closer to some higher mystery, or truth. Ultimately, however West's fascination with those on trial has less to do with philosophy than with morality and compassion. Always her effort is to see (and make us see) that these demons are men, and that whatever we might learn from them and their crimes will be lost to us if we insist on assigning them to some other species. She reminds us that "if a trial for murder lasts too long, more than the murder will out. The man in the murderer will out; it becomes horrible to think of destroying him." She describes the Nazi war criminals as they are about to be sentenced:

> Their pale, lined faces looked alike, their bodies sagged inside their clothes, which seemed more alive than they were. They were gone. They were finished. It seemed strange that they could ever have excited loyalty, it was plainly impossible that they could ever attract it again.... They were not abject. These ghosts gathered about them the rags of what had been good

in them during their lives. They listened with decent composure to the reading of the judgements, and, as on any other day, they found amusement in the judges pronunciation of the German names. That is something pitiable which those who do not attend trials never see: the eagerness with which people in the dock snatch at any occasion for laughter.

West is present in the courtroom when the men are told they are going be hanged. "No wise person," she asserts, "will write an unnecessary word about hanging, for fear of straying into the field of pornography." Yet she concludes the first part of "Greenhouse with Cyclamens" with a bloodcurdling disquisition on the history of this form of execution, a description of the eleven condemned men slowly choking to death and of Ribbentrop struggling in the air for twenty minutes before finally expiring. Of course she believes that the Nazis, those "abcesses of cruelty" deserved to be punished—though she feels the act of execution further extends the long trajectory of cruelty and death. Ultimately, West's faith in justice transcends the predicament of the individual criminal and the seriousness of his crime. She is less concerned with the pathology of the condemned than with the collective health of whole communities, countries, civilization—entities that, in her

view, are also on trial in these proceedings. It's not the cruelty of hanging that alarms her so much as what that cruelty can trigger in human nature: "For when society has to hurt a man it must hurt him as little as possible and must preserve what it can of his pride, lest there should spread in that society those feelings which make men do the things for which they get hanged."

This astonishing book makes us long to know what Rebecca West would have made of the trials of O.J. Simpson, Susan Smith and the Menendez brothers—all the grisly mass entertainments, these gory cock fights staged on a colossal scale—that we have come to accept as legitimate legal procedures on which men and women's lives depend. *A Train of Powder* makes us look harder to see what she might have seen: her flashes of insight into the minds of criminals and victims, her long gaze into the future to discern the distant shock waves, the social repercussions of these sensational trials and the ways in which justice is served or betrayed. How terrible that it should be out of print, this book that makes us pay a different sort of attention to the legal battles that periodically turn our living rooms, our offices, our neighborhood barber shops and bars into annexes of the courtrooms on which all the rest depends.

KATE BRAVERMAN

FRAN GORDON

Twice nominated for a Pulitzer, this vastly underappreciated apocalyptic poet is also, as Rick Moody calls her, "one of the great American systemizers of obsession and revelation in prose." Her first novel, *Lithium for Medea*, a cult classic, was published in 1979. At a time of minimalist misanthropy, Braverman's voice, laden with pregnant language and humanity, was the powerful one. And in this time of timid passions, it still is. Braverman's style skates on decadence but virtuosity propels it. Her women remain unprecedented; they risk but do not regret. They are chance survivors, societal drop outs, settlers of the border region between loneliness and man.

Braverman lived under a table with her works for almost a year; when she slept, it was on her typewriter. Her O'Henry winner, "Tall Tales from the Mekong Delta," manifests the specter of addiction like no other story. In sobriety, Braverman has lost none of her edge. In fact, she sees the chasm with a stunning new clarity. The progeny of her squanderers have come into focus. They deal with their ailing world with aplomb, while Braverman hangs a bowed blue backdrop to illuminate its threat. The adolescent bent in her new collection, *Small Craft Warnings*, was largely ignored by *The New York Times Book Review*, which referred to it as "stories about women abandoned by men." These men recede but Braverman's women leave. They are amongst the most mobile characters in contemporary fiction. The same review finds the stories' tautologies an "annoyance," but obsession is by definition repetitive, and yes, Braverman is excessive. "I'm going to live in the woods and stalk story," she said. She couldn't understand what hers had to do with critics. And so she left.

·　·　·　·　·

Kate Braverman lives with her family in the northern Allegheny mountain region of New York. Small Craft Warnings (Western Literature Series) is available through University of Nevada Press. Her award-winning backlist, out-of-print, is available with minimal wait through Amazon.com.

THE FINAL OPUS OF LEON SOLOMON

HELEN SCHULMAN

If being out of print is a little like death for a writer—or at least for the text, which is unable to make new attachments and fades slowly from the memory of those who adored it—is the desire to get a book back into print akin to the desire to bring a friend back to life? I think this as I pore over *The Final Opus of Leon Solomon*, a novel by the late Jerome Badanes, published by Knopf in 1989 and now unavailable. Do I want this book sent back to press simply because I long to see the bearded, wise-eyed Badanes lumbering down Broadway? Sure, and no. It is one of the best Holocaust novels I have read. Badanes's strength lies not only in his perfect prose, but in his boldness in describing

> *Is the desire to get a book back into print akin to the desire to bring a friend back to life?*

a troubled life, Leon Solomon's, interrupted by historical atrocities so brutal they are still, at this late date, hard for the mind to accept. Instead of the cliché of a picture-perfect Sabbath dinner disrupted by storm troopers, Badanes paints a rich and disturbing portrait of an already tattered family further unraveling as it faces annihilation. The scene in which the love of Leon Solomon's life—his sister—is beaten to death is one of the most harrowing paragraphs in literature. For readers, the dreadful toll of living alongside Leon Solomon is balanced by the deeper understanding we gain of what it means to survive after everything is lost. To survive half dead. And thus we find ourselves changed, as people, in ways both tangible and mysterious, after turning the final pages. Isn't that why we read? How I wish more of us could get our hands on this one.

UP THE JUNCTION

RACHEL RESNICK

Published in 1963, *Up the Junction* is still fresh as a dandelion pushing through dirty concrete, trampled clippity-clop by a red sling-back high heel. Only twenty-seven at the time of publication, Nell Dunn, an "heiress from Chelsea" with a background in journalism, plunked down in Battersea for a bit of behind-the-flanks reportage. The result was pure alchemy. After the collection of stories came out (four were originally published in Britain's *New Statesman*), Ken Loach directed a BBC dramatization in 1965 and in 1967, Peter Collinson directed a movie version. In 1990, Penguin USA put out a paperback edition under their Virago Modern Classics imprint. Today it's out of print—a true shame. *Up The Junction* is gorgeously visceral. It kicks. It breathes. It giggles. You can taste the fat chips dipped in egg yolk, hear the rumble of lorries, see the girls in their beehives, smell the beery wonder of packed pubs. Even Dunn's modern taste for naming consumer goods—word-chewables like Babycham, Spangles, Daz, Saxa and Kit-E-Kat—only adds to the book's texture rather than dating it. But more than all this, peoples' lives MATTER. They sweat, they eat, they love, they fight, they bleed. Through the clear, virtually egoless eye of the narrator, you meet what feels like the whole bloody neighborhood in the space of 110 perfect pages: witness cheeky come-ons, reckless burn-ups that end in violent and untimely death, snogging sessions in bombed-out sites, shopping trips up the junction, clipjoint hustles, petty thieving, and frank sex talk among birds and blokes alike—all done with high-voltage language that will light you up like a Belisha beacon. Flannery O'Connor predicted that the novel would edge closer and closer to poetry. *Up The Junction* is a sweaty, sexy, working-class incarnation of that prophecy. If you're lucky enough to find it, used, this book will charm yer knickers off. ▮

> *'Up the Junction' is gorgeously visceral. It kicks. It breathes. It giggles. You can taste the fat chips dipped in egg yolk, hear the rumble of lorries, see the girls in their beehives, smell the beery wonder of packed pubs.*

THE GAY PLACE

BY JIM LEWIS

When Billy Lee Brammer published *The Gay Place*, in 1961, he meant it to be a novel of politics rather than a political novel; the idea of 'identity' was still in its infant stage, and the paranoid style was yet to come. All Brammer wanted was to describe some days among the Texas state legislators in the late 1950s, and he did so with great style and grace, and with the melancholy of a young man getting notice-

———•———

There is life in 'The Gay Place,' which is a rare enough thing to find in a novel; there is politics, which is rarer; and there is art, which is rarer still.

———•———

ably older by the day. They still remember the book down around Austin; they've hardly heard of it anywhere else. The author never wrote another, and he died of a drug overdose in the mid-seventies.

Brammer worked as an aide to LBJ in Texas, and a mythic Johnson—renamed Arthur Fenstemaker and situated in the governor's mansion rather than D.C.—looms over the scene, plotting, manipulating, joking, blustering, intoning, drinking, fornicating, holding forth with his inimitable tang. Fenstemaker plays Big Daddy, and he's at once admired and resented by the three protagonists of the book's three concatenated novellas: a state legislator, a speechwriter, and a first-term U.S. senator, all of whom have a slightly callow, romantic, Fitzgeraldian fatalism. They're a postwar Lost Generation of Bubbas, if you can imagine such a thing.

For some time, among some people, *The Gay Place* was considered the second-best novel of American politics, after *All the King's Men*, which, by my lights, it betters. But since politics—I mean real, school-bill, caucus-vote, precinct-boss politics—has fallen out of aesthetic favor in this godforsaken nation, only Warren's book survives, and then only as a kind of quaint curiosity. It's a shame, really, because there is life in *The Gay Place*, which is a rare enough thing to find in a novel; there is politics, which is rarer; and there is art, which is rarer still. ▪

POSSUM LIVING

DAVID GATES

I found Dolly Freed's *Possum Living* (Universe Books, 1978) in the attic of the fixer-upper farmhouse I bought in 1985, along with a stack of Sunset books on such topics as building decks and preserving vegetables. The previous owners had been utopians, too. Its grocery-bag brown covers and faux-typewriter typeface fit the post-hippie, Carter-era gestalt suggested by the subtitle: "How to Live Well Without a Job and with [the word almost careted in] No Money." It advocates a life of quasi-Beckettian simplicity: foraging in supermarket Dumpsters, burning scrap wood and dead branches in woodstoves homemade from oil drums, raising rabbits in the basement ("We take close to 300 pounds of meat out of that cellar per year"). What makes all this refreshing is Freed's utter lack of high-mindedness. "We live this way for a very simple reason: It's easier to learn to do without some of the things that money can buy than to earn the money to buy them. . . . So if you're thinking spiritual or sociological thoughts, don't waste your time with me."

Supposedly Freed was nineteen years old when she wrote this, living with her divorced father, aka the Old Fool, in a Philadelphia suburb. Here and there she gives glimpses of a rancorous, downwardly mobile, borderline-violent milieu like that of her contemporary Raymond Carver. "A friend of ours," she notes in passing, in a chapter on "everyday nitty-gritty law," "lost his cool and threatened his wife's lawyer in open court." She goes on to advise better methods of bringing an "adversary" to reason: "Visit his house late at night and do something to let him know he has an enemy who has no intention of playing the game by his rules." Among Freed's broad hints: cut his phone line, poison his dog. The dark stories she never quite tells and her even-handed contempt both for the culture of acquisition and consumption and for ecopuritan ideology make *Possum Living* one of the out-of-control classics of American cantankerousness, like *Walden, ABC of Economics, Steal This Book!* and *The Closing of the American Mind*. It directly inspired parts of my first novel, *Jernigan*: my protagonist's girlfriend raises bunnies and reads a magazine called *Suburban Survivalist*. I credited *Possum Living* in my acknowledgments, but never heard from Dolly Freed. That was back in 1991; both my dog and my phone line are still okay.

ON HIS DEATHBED, HOLDING YOUR HAND, THE ACCLAIMED <small>NEW</small> NEW YOUNG OFF-BROADWAY <small>FICTION</small> PLAYWRIGHT'S <small>FROM</small> FATHER BEGS A BOON

DAVID FOSTER WALLACE

[46]

THE FATHER: Listen: I did despise him. Do.

[PAUSE for episode of ophthalmorrhagia; technician's swab/flush of dextrocular orbit; change of bandage]

THE FATHER: Why does no one tell you? Why do all regard it as a blessed event? There seems to be almost a conspiracy to keep you in the dark. Why does no one take you aside and tell you what is coming? Why not tell you the truth? That your life is to be forfeit? That you are expected now to give up everything and not only to receive no thanks but to expect none? Not one. To suspend the essential give-and-take you'd spent years learning was life and now want nothing? I tell you, worse than nothing: that you will have no more life that is *yours*? That all you wished for yourself you are now expected to wish for him instead? Whence this expectation? Does it sound reasonable to expect? Of a human being? To have nothing and wish nothing for *you*? That your entire human nature should somehow change, alter, as if magically, at the moment it emerges from her after causing her such pain and deforming her body so profoundly that ne—that she will herself somehow alter herself this way automatically, as if by magic, the instant he emerges, as if by some glandular bewitchment, but that you, who have not carried him or been joined by tubes, will remain, inside, as you have always been, yet be expected to change as well, drop everything, freely? Why does no one speak of it, this madness? That your failure to cast yourself away and change everything and be delirious with joy at—that this will be judged. Not just as a quote unquote parent but as a man. Your human worth. The prim smug look of those who would judge parents, judge them for not magically changing, not instantly ceding everything you'd wished for heretofore and—*securus judicat orbis terrarum*, Father. But Father are we really to believe it is so obvious and natural that no one feels even any *need* to tell you? Instinctive as blinking? Never think to warn you? It did not seem obvious to me, I can assure you. Have you ever actually seen an afterbirth? watch drop-jawed and unblinking as it emerged and hit the floor, and what they do with it? No one told me I assure you. That one's own wife might judge you deficient simply for remaining the man she married. Was I the only one not told? Why such silence when—

[PAUSE for episode of dyspnea]

THE FATHER: I despised him from the first. I do not exaggerate. From the first

NO ONE PREPARED US FOR ANY OF IT, FOR THE SHEER UNPLEASANTNESS OF IT. THE INSANE EXPENSE OF PASTEL PLASTIC THINGS. THE CLOACAL REEK OF THE NURSERY. THE ENDLESS LAUNDRY. THE ODORS AND CONSTANT NOISE. THE DISRUPTION OF ALL POSSIBLE SCHEDULE.

moment they finally saw fit to let me in and I looked down and saw him already attached to her, already sucking away. Sucking at her, draining her, and her upturned face—she who had made her views on the sucking of body parts very plain, I can—her face, she had changed, become an abstraction, The Mother, her natal face enraptured, radiant, as if nothing invasive or grotesque were taking place. She had screamed on the table, *screamed*, and now where was that girl? I had never seen her look so—the current term is 'out of it,' no? Has anyone considered this phrase? what it really implies? In that instant I knew I despised him. There is no other word. Despicable. The whole affair from then on. The truth: I found it neither natural nor fulfilling nor beautiful nor fair. Think of me what you will. It is the truth. It was all disgusting. Ceaseless. The sensory assault. You cannot know. The incontinence. The vomit. The sheer smell. The noise. The theft of sleep. The selfishness, the appalling selfishness of the newborn, you have no idea. No one prepared us for any of it, for the sheer unpleasantness of it. The insane expense of pastel plastic things. The cloacal reek of the nursery. The endless laundry. The odors and constant noise. The disruption of all possible schedule. The slobber and terror and piercing shrieks. Like a needle those shrieks. Perhaps if someone had prepared, forewarned us. The endless reconfiguration of all schedules around him. Around his desires. He ruled from that crib, ruled from the first. Ruled her, reduced and remade her. Even as an infant the power he wielded! I learned the bottomless greed of him. Of my son. Of arrogance past imagining. The regal greed and thoughtless disorder and mindless cruelty—the literal *thoughtlessness* of him. Has anyone considered this phrase's real import? Of the *thoughtlessness* with which he treated the world? The way he threw things aside and clutched at things, the way he broke things and just walked away. As a toddler. Terrible Twos indeed. I watched other children; I studied other children his age—something in him was different, missing. Psychotic, sociopathic. The grotesque lack of care for what we gave him. Believe me. You were of course forbidden to say 'I paid for that! Treat that with care! Show some minim of respect for something outside yourself!' No never that. Never that. You'd be a monster. What sort of parent asks for a moment's thought to whence things came? Never. Not a thought. I spent years drop-jawed with amazement, too appalled even to know what—noplace to speak of it. No one else even appeared to see it. Him. An

essential disorder of character. An absence of whatever we mean by 'human.' A psychosis no one dares diagnose. No one says it—that you are to live for and serve a psychotic. No one mentions the abuse of power. No one mentions that there will be psychotic tantrums during which you will wish—even just his face, I did, I detested his face. He had a small soft moist face, not human. A circle of cheese with features like hasty pinches in some ghastly dough. Am—was I the only one? That an infant's face is not in any way recognizable, not a human face—it's true—then why do all clasp their hands and call it beauty? Why not simply admit to an ugliness that may well be outgrown? Why such—but the way from the beginning his eye—my son's right eye—it protruded, subtly yes, slightly more than the left, and blinked in a palsied and overrapid way, like the sputter of a defective circuit. That fluttery blinking. The subtle but once noticed never thenceforth ignorable bulge of that same eye. Its subtle but aggressive forward thrust. All was to be his, that eye betrayed the—a triumph in it, a glazed exultation. Pediatric term was 'exophthalmic,' supposedly harmless, correctable over time. I never told her what I knew: not correctable, not an accidental sign. That was the eye to look at, into it, if you wished to see what no one else wished to see or acknowledge. The mask's only gap. Hear this. I loathed my child. I loathed the eye, the mouth, the lip, the pinched snout, the wet hanging lip. His very skin was an affliction. 'Impetigo' the term, chronic. The pediatricians could find no reason. The insurance a nightmare. I spent half my days on the phone with these people. Wearing a mask of concern to match hers. Never a word. A sickly child, weak and cheese-white, chronically congested. The suppurating sores of his chronic impetigo, the crust. The ruptured infections. 'Suppuration': the term means ooze. My son oozed, exuded, flaked, suppurated, dribbled from every quadrant. To whom does one speak of this? That he taught me to despise the body, what it is to have a body—to be disgusted, repulsed. Often I had to look away, duck outside, dart around corners. The absent thoughtless picking and scratching and probing and toying, bottomless narcissistic fascination with his own body. As if his extremities were the world's four corners. A slave to himself. An engine of mindless will. A reign of terror, trust me. The insane tantrums when his will was thwarted. When some gratification was denied or delayed. It was Kafkan—you were punished for protecting him from himself. 'No, no, child, my son, I cannot allow you to thrust your hand into the vaporizer's hot water, the blades of the window fan, do not drink that household solvent'—a tantrum. The insanity of it. You could not explain or reason. You could only walk away appalled. Will yourself not simply to let him the next time, not to smile and let him, 'Have at that solvent, my son,' learn the hard way. The whining and wheedling and tugging and towering rages. Not really psychotic, I came to see. Crazy like a fox. An agenda behind every outburst. 'Too much excitement, overtired, cranky, feverish, needs a lie-down, just frustrated, just a long day'—the litany of her excuses for him. His endless emotional manipulation of her. The ceaselessness of it and her inhuman reaction: even when she recognized what he was up to she excused him, she was charmed by the nakedness of his insecurity, his what she called 'need' for her, what she called my son's 'need for reassurance.' Need for reassurance? What reassurance? He never doubted. He knew it all belonged to him. He never doubted. As if it were due him. As if he deserved it. Insanity. Solipsism. He wanted it all. All I had, had had, never would. It never ended. Blind, reasonless appetite. I will say it: evil. There. I can imagine your face. But he was evil. And I alone seemed to know it. He afflicted me in a thousand ways and I could say nothing.

My face fairly ached at day's end from the control I was forced to exert over—even the slight note of complaint you could hear in his breathing. The bruised circles of restless appetite beneath his eyes. Exhalation a whimper. The two different eyes, the one terrible eye. The redness and flaccidity of his mouth and the way the lip was always wet no matter how much one wiped it for him. An inherently moist child, always clammy, the scent of him vaguely fungal. The vacancy of his face when he became absorbed in some pleasure. The utter shamelessness of his greed. The sense of utter entitlement. How long it took us to teach him even a perfunctory thank you. And he never meant it, and she did not mind. She would—never minded. She was his servant. Slave mentality. This was not the girl I asked to marry me. She was his slave and

believed she knew only joy. He played with her as a cat does a toy mouse and she felt joy. Madness? Where was my wife? What was this creature she stroked as he sucked at her? Most of his childhood— memory of it— most renders down to seeing myself standing there some yards away, watching them in appalled amazement. Behind my dutiful smile. Too weak ever to speak out, to ask it. This was my life. This is the truth I've hidden. You are good to listen. More important than you know. To speak it. *Te ju*—judge me as you wish. No, do. I am dying—no, I know—bedridden, near blind, gutted, catarrh, dying, alone and in pain. Look at these bloody tubes. All these tubes. A life of such silence. And this is my confession. Good of you. Not what you—it is not your forgiveness I—just to hear the truth. About him. That I despised

> AN INHERENTLY MOIST CHILD, ALWAYS CLAMMY, THE SCENT OF HIM VAGUELY FUNGAL. THE VACANCY OF HIS FACE WHEN HE BECAME ABSORBED IN SOME PLEASURE. THE UTTER SHAMELESSNESS OF HIS GREED.

him. There is no other word. Often I was forced to avert my eyes from him, look away. Hide. I discovered why fathers hold the evening paper as they do.

[PAUSE for FATHER's attempted pantomime of holding object spread before face]

THE FATHER: I am recalling now just one in un—something, a tantrum over something or other after dinner one evening. I did not want him eating in our living room. Not unreasonable I think. The dining room was for eating; I had explained to him the etymology and sense of *'dining room.'* The living room, where I reserved for myself but half an hour with the news-paper after dinner—and there he was, sud-denly right there before me, on the new carpet, eating his candy in the living room. Was I unreasonable? He had received the candy as his reward for eating the healthy dinner I had worked to buy for him and she had worked to prepare for him—feel it? the judgment, disgust? that one is never to say such a thing, to mention that one paid, that one's limited resources had been devoted to—that would be selfish, no? a bad par-ent, no? niggardly? *selfish?* And yet I had, had paid for the little colored chocolate candies, candies which here he stood upending the little bag to be able to get all of the candy into that mouth at once, never one by one, always all the sweets all at once, as much as fast as possible regardless of spillage, hence my gritted smile and carefully gentle reminder of the etymology of *'dining* room' and far less a command than—mindful of her reaction, always—*request* that, please, no candy in the—and with his mouth crammed with candy and chewing at it even as the tantrum began, puling and stamping his feet and shrieking now at the top of his lungs in the living room even as his mouth was filled with chocolate, that open red mouth filled with mashed candy which mixed with his spittle and as he howled overran his lip as he howled and stamped up and down and running down his chin and shirt, and peer-ing timidly over the top of the paper held like a shield as I sat willing myself to remain in the chair and say nothing and watching now his mother down on one knee trying to wipe the chocolate drool off his chin as he screamed at her and batted the napkin away. Who could look on this and not be appalled? Who could—when was it determined that this sort of thing is acceptable, that such a creature must be not only tolerated no but *soothed*, actually *placated*, as she was on her knees doing, tenderly, in gross contradiction to the unac-ceptability of what was going on. What sort of madness is this? That I can hear the soft little singsong tones she used to try to soothe him—for *what*?—as she patiently brings the napkin back again and again as he bats it away and screams that he hates her. I do not exaggerate; he said this: hates her. *Hates* her? *Her*? Down on one knee, pretending she hears nothing, that it's nothing, cranky, long day, that—what bewitchment lay behind this patience? What human being could remain on her knees wiping drool caused by *his*, *his* violation of a simple and reasonable prohibition against just this very sort of disgusting mess in the room in which we sought only to *live*? What chasm of insanity lay between us? What was this creature? Why did we go on like this? How might I be in any way culpable for lifting the evening paper to try to obscure this scene? It was either look away or kill him where he stood. How does doing what must be done to control my— how is this equal to my being remote or ungiving unquote or heaven forfend 'cruel'? Cruel to *that*? Why is 'cruel' applied only to those who pay for the little chocolates he spews onto the shirtfront you paid for to dribble onto the carpet you paid for and grinds under the shoes you paid for as he stamps up and down in mindless fury at your mild request that he take reasonable steps to avert precisely the sort of mess he

is causing? Am I the only one to whom this makes no sense? who is revolted, appalled? Why is even to speak of such revulsion not allowed? Who made this rule? Why was it I who must be seen and not heard? Whence this inversion of my own upbringing? What unthinkable discipline would my own father have—

[PAUSE for episode of dyspnea, blennorrhagia]

THE FATHER: Did. Sometimes I did, no, literally could not bear the sight of him. Impetigo is a skin disorder. His scalp's sores suppurated and formed a crust. The crust then turned yellow. A childhood skin disease. Condition of children. When he coughed it rained yellow crust. His bad eye wept constantly, a viscous stuff that has no name. His eyelashes at the breakfast his mother made would be clotted with a pale crust which someone would have to clean off with a swab while he writhed in complaint at being cleaned of repellent crust. About him hung a scent of spoilage, mildew. And she would nuzzle just to smell him. Nose running without cease or reason and caused small red raised sores on his nostrils and upper lip which then yielded more crust. Chronic ear infections meant not only a spike in the incidence of tantrums but an actual smell, a discharge whose odor I will spare you describing. Antibiotics. He was a veritable petri dish of infection and discharge and eruption and runoff, white as a root, blotched, moist, like something in a cellar. And yet all who saw him clasped their hands together and exclaimed. Beautiful child. Angel. Soulful. Delicate. Break such hearts. The word 'beautiful' was used. I would simply stand there—what could I say? My carefully pleased expression. But could they have seen that inhuman little puke-white face during an infection, an attack, a tantrum, the piggy malevolence of it, the truculent entitlement, the rapacity. The ugliness. 'Barked about most lazar-like with vile'—the ugly truth. Mucus, pus, vomit, feces, diarrhea, urine, wax, sputum, varicolored crusts. These were his dowry to—the gifts he bore us. Thrashing in sleep or fever, clutching at the very air as if to pull it to him. And always there bedside she was, his, in thrall, bewitched, wiping and swabbing and stroking and tending, never a word of acknowledgment of the sheer horror of what he produced and expected her to wipe away. The endless thankless expectation. Never acknowledged. The girl I married would have reacted very, very differently to this creature, believe me. Treating her breasts as if they were his. Property.

HE WAS A VERITABLE PETRI DISH OF INFECTION AND DISCHARGE AND ERUPTION AND RUNOFF, WHITE AS A ROOT, BLOTCHED, MOIST, LIKE SOMETHING IN A CELLAR. AND YET ALL WHO SAW HIM CLASPED THEIR HANDS TOGETHER AND EXCLAIMED. BEAUTIFUL CHILD. ANGEL.

Her nipples the color of a skinned knee. Grasping, clutching. Making greedy sounds. Manhandling her. Snorting, wheezing. Absorbed wholly in his own sensations. Reflectionless. At home in his body as only one whose body is not *his* job can be at home. Filled with himself, right to the edges like a swollen pond. He was his body. I often could not look. Even the speed of his growth that first year—statistically unusual, the doctors remarked it—a rate that was weedy, aggressive, a willed imposition of self on space. That right eye's sputtering forward thrust. Sometimes she would grimace at the weight of him, holding him, lifting, until she caught the brief grimace and wiped it away—I was sure I saw it—replaced at once with that expression of narcotic patience, abstract thrall, I several yards off, extrorse, trying not—

[PAUSE for episode of dyspnea; technician's application of tracheobronchial suction catheter]

THE FATHER: Never learned to breathe is why. Awful of me to say, yes? And of course yes ironic, given—and she'd have died on the spot to hear me say it. But it is the truth. Some chronic asthma and a tendency to bronchitis, yes, but that is not what I—I mean nasal. Nothing structurally wrong with his nose. Paid several times to

have it examined, probed, they all concurred, nose normal, most of the occlusion from simple disuse. Chronic disuse. The truth: he never bothered to learn. Through it. Why bother? Breathed through his mouth, which is of course easier in the short term, requires less effort, maximizes intake, get it all in at once. And does, my son, breathes to this very day through his slack and much-loved adult mouth, which consequently is always partly open, this mouth, slack and wet, and white bits of rancid froth collect at the corners and are of course too much trouble ever to check in a lavatory mirror and attend to discreetly in private and spare others the sight of the pellets of paste at the corners of his mouth, forcing everyone to say nothing and pretend they do not see. The equivalent of long, unclean, or long nails on men, which I tirelessly tried to explain were in his own best interest to keep trimmed and clean. When I picture him it is always with his mouth partly open and lower lip wet and hanging and projecting outward far further than a lower lip ought, one eye dull with greed and the other's palsied bulge. This sounds ugly? It was ugly. Blame the messenger. Do. Silence me. Say the word. Verily, Father, but whose ugliness? Are we certain? For is she—that he was a sickly child as a child who—always in bed with asthma or ears, constant bronchitis and upper flu, slight chronic asthma yes true but bed for days at a time when some sun and fresh air could not poss—ring for, hurts—he had a little silver bell by the rocket's snout he'd ring, to summon her. Not a normal regular child's bed but a catalogue bed, battleship gray they called Authentic Silvery Finish plus Postage and Handling with aerodynamic booster fins and snout, assembly required and the instructions practically Cyrillic and yes and whom do you suppose was expec—the little silver tinkle of the bell and she'd fly, fly to him, bending uncomfortably over the booster fins of the bed, cold iron fins, minist—it rang and rang.

[PAUSE for episode of ophthalmorrhagia; technician's swab/flush of dextrocular orbit; change of facial bandage]

THE FATHER: Bells of course employed throughout history to summon servants, domestics, an observation I kept to myself when she got him the bell. The official version was that the bell was to be used if he could not breathe, in lieu of calling out. It was to be an emergency bell. But he abused it. Whenever he was ill he continually rang the bell. Sometimes just to force her to come sit next to the bed. Her presence was demanded and off she went. Even in sleep, if the bell rang, however softly, slyly, sounding more like a wish than a ring, she would hear it and be out of bed and off down the hall without even putting on her robe. The hall was often cold. House poorly insulated and ferociously dear to heat. I, when I awoke, would take her her robe, slippers; she never thought of them. To see her arise still asleep at that maddening tinkle was to see mind control at its most elemental. This was his genius: to *need*. The sleep he robbed her of, at will, daily, for years.

> # TO SEE HER ARISE STILL ASLEEP AT THAT MADDENING TINKLE WAS TO SEE MIND CONTROL AT ITS MOST ELEMENTAL. THIS WAS HIS GENIUS: TO NEED.

Watching her face and body fall. Her body never had the chance to recover. Sometimes she looked like an old woman. Ghastly circles under her eyes. Legs swollen. He took years from her. And she'd have sworn she gave them freely. Sworn it. I'm not speaking now of *my* sleep, *my* life. He never thought of her except in reference to himself. This is the truth. I know him. If you had seen him at the funeral. As a child he—she'd hear the bell and without even coming fully awake pad off to the lavatory and turn on every faucet and fill the place with steam and sit for hours holding him on the commode in the steam while he slept—that he made her trade her own rest for his, night after—and that not only was all the hot water for all of us for the entire next morning exhausted but the constant steam then would infiltrate upstairs and everything was constantly sodden with his steam and in warm weathers came a rank odor of mold which she would have been appalled had I openly credited to him as its real source, his rocket and tinkle, all wood everywhere warping, wallpaper peeling off in sheets. The gifts he bestowed. That Christmas film—their joke was that he was giving angels wings each time. It was not that he was not sometimes truly ill, it would not be true to accuse him of—but he *used* it. The bell was only one of the more obvious—and she believed it was all her idea. To orbit him. To alter, cede herself. Vanish as a person. To become an abstraction: The Mother, Down On One Knee. This was life after he came—she orbits him, I chart her movements. That she could call him a blessing, the sun in her sky. She was no more the girl I'd married. And she never knew how I missed that girl, mourned her, how my heart went out to what she'd become. I was weak not to tell her the truth. Despised him. Couldn't. This was the insidious part, the part I truly despised, that he ruled *me*, as well, despite my seeing through him. I could not help it. After he came some chasm lay between us. My voice could not carry across it. How often on so many late nights I would lean weakly in the doorway of the lavatory wiping steam from my spectacles with the belt of the robe and was so desperate to say it, to utter it: 'What about *us*? Where had our lives gone? Why did this choking sucking thankless thing mean more than we? Who had decided that this should be so?' Beg her to come out of it, snap out. In despair, weak, not utter—she would not have heard me. That is why not. Afraid that what she would hear would—hear only a bad father, deficient man, uncaring, *selfish*, and then the last of the freely chosen bonds between us would be severed. That she would choose. Weak. Oh I was doomed and knew it. My self-respect was a plaything in those clammy little hands as well. The *genius* of his weakness. Nietzsche had no *idea*. Ballocks all reason for—and this, this was my thank-you— free tickets? A black joke. *Free* he calls them? And airfare to come and applaud and shape my face's grin to pretend with the rest of—*this* is my thank-you? Oh the endless sense of entitlement. Endless. That you understand eternal doom in all the late-night sickly hours forced in a one-buttock hunch on the booster's bolted fin of the ridiculous rocket-shaped bed he cajoled her—more plaything than bed, impossible instructions on my knees with the wrong tool as he stood in my light— ironized fin no broader than a ham but I'm damned if I'll kneel by that ill-assembled bed. My job to maintain the vaporizer and administer wet cloths and monitor the breathing and fever as he lay holding the bell while again she was off unrested out in the cold to the all-night druggist to hunch there on the booster-stage fin awash in the odor of mentholate gel and yawning and checking my watch and looking down at him resting with wet mouth agape and watching the chest make its diffident minimal effort of rising and falling while

he through the flutter of that right lid staring without expression or making one acknowledgment of—rising then up out of an almost oneiric reverie to realize that I had been wishing it to cease, that chest, to still its sluggish movement under the Gemini comforter he demanded to have upon him at—dreaming of it falling still, stilled, the bell to cease its patrician tinkle, the last rattle of that weak and omnipotent chest, and yes I would then strike my own breast, crosswise thus—

[FATHER's weak pantomime of striking own chest]

—in punishment of my wish, ashamed, such was my own thrall to him. He merely staring up slackly at my self-abuse, with that red wet lip hanging wetly, rancid froth, lazar-like crust, chin's spittle, chest's unguent's menthol reek, a creamy little gout of snot protruding, that blank eye sputtering like a bad bulb—put it out! put it out!

[PAUSE for technician's removal, cleaning, reinsertion of O₂ feed into FATHER's nostril]

THE FATHER: That cramped on that fin and dabbing tender at his forehead and wiping away some of the chin's sputum and sitting gazing at it on the handkerchief, trying to—and—yes at the pillow, looking at the pillow, gazing at the pillow and thought of it, how quickly it—how few movements required not just to wish but to will it, to impose my own will as he so blithely always did, lying there pretending to be too feverish to see my—but it was, it was pathetic, not even—I was thinking of my weight on the pillow as a man in arrears thinks of sudden fortune, sweepstakes, inheritance. Wishful thinking. I believed then that I was struggling with my will, but it was mere fantasy. Not will. Aquinas's velleity. I lacked whatever it seems to take to be able to—or perhaps I failed to lack what must be lacking, yes? I could not have. Wishing it but not—both decency *and* weakness perhaps. *Te judice*, Father, yes? I know I was weak. But listen: I did wish it. That is no confession but just the truth. I did wish it. I did despise him. I did miss her and mourn. I did resent—I failed to see why his weakness should permit him to win. It was insane, made no sense—on the basis of what merit or capacity should *he* win? And she never knew. This was the worst, his *lèse-majesté*, unforgivable: the chasm he opened between her and I. My unending pretense. My fear that she'd think me a monster, deficient. I pretended to love him as she did. This I confess. I subjected her to a—the last twenty-nine years of our life together were a lie. My lie. She never

knew. I could pretend with the best of them. No adulterer was more careful a dissembler than I. I would help her off with her wrap and take the small sack from the druggist's and whisper my earnest little report on the state of his breathing and temperature throughout her absence, she listening but looking past me, at him, not noting how perfectly my expression's concern matched her own. I modeled my face on hers; she taught me to pretend. It never even occurred to her. Can you understand what this did to me? That she never for a moment doubted I felt the same, that I ceded myself as—that I too was under the sucking thing's spell?

[PAUSE for episode of severe dyspnea; R.N.'s application of tracheobronchial suction catheter]

THE FATHER: That she never thenceforth knew me? That my wife had ceased to know me? That I let her go and pretended to join her? Might I hope that anyone could imagine the—

[PAUSE for episode of ocular bobbing; technician's flush/evacuation of ophthalmorrhagic residue; change of ocular bandage]

THE FATHER: That we would make love and afterward lie curled together in our special position preparing to sleep and she'd not be still, whispering on and on about him, every conceivable ephemera about him, worries and wishes, a mother's prattle—and took my silence for agreement. The chasm's essence was that she believed there was no chasm. Our bed's width grew day by day and she never—not once occurred to her. That I saw through and loathed him. That I not merely failed to share her bewitchment but was appalled by it. It was my fault, not hers. I tell you this: he was the only secret I had from her. She was the very sun in my sky. The loneliness of the secret was an agony past—oh I loved her so. My feelings for her never wavered. I loved her from the first. We were meant to be together. Joined, united. I knew it the moment— saw her there on the arm of that Bowdoin twit in his fur collar. Holding her pennant as one would a parasol. That I cathected her on the spot. I had a bit of an accent then; she twitted me for it. She would impersonate me when I was cross—only your life's one love could do this—the anger would vanish. The way she affected me. She followed American football and had a son who could not play and then later when he mysteriously ceased being sickly and grew sleek and vigorous would not play. She went instead to watch him

swim. The nauseous diminutives, Wuggums, Tigerbear. He swam in public school. The stink of cheap bleach in the venues, barely breathe. Did she miss even one event? When did she stop following it, the football on the misaligned Zenith we would watch together—hold it still, the— making love and lying curled like twins in the womb, saying everything. I could tell her anything. When did that all go then. Just when did he take it from us. Why can't I remember. I remember the day we met as if it were yesterday but I'm bollixed if I can remember yesterday. Pathetic, disgusting. They do not care but if they knew what it—felt to hurt to bloody breathe. Enwebbed in tubes. Bastards, bleeding out every—yes I saw her and she me, the demurely held pennant I was new over and could not parse—our eyes met, all the clichés came instantly true—I knew she was the one to have all of me. A spotlight followed her across the lawn. I simply knew. Father, this was the acme of my life. Watching—that 'she was the girl for all of me / my unworthy life for thee' [melody unfamiliar, discordant]. To stand before Church and man and pledge it. To unwrap one another like gifts from God. Conversation's lifetime. If you could have seen her on our wedding—no of course not, that look as she—for me alone. To love at such depth. No better feeling in all creation. She would cock her head just so when amused. So much used to amuse her. We laughed at everything. We were our secret. She chose me. One another. I told her things I had not told my own brother. We belonged to one another. I felt chosen. Who chose *him,* pray? Who gave informed consent to everything hitherto's loss? I despised him for forcing me to hide the fact the fact that I despised him. The common run is one thing, with their judgments, the demand to see you dandle and coo and toss the ball. But her? That I must wear this mask for her? Sounds monstrous but it's true: his fault. I simply couldn't. Tell her. That I—that he was in truth loathsome. That I so bitterly regretted letting her conceive. That she did not truly see him. To trust me, that she was under a spell, lost to herself. That she must come back. That I missed her so. None. And not for my sake, believe—she could not have borne it. It would have destroyed her. She'd have been destroyed, and on his account. He did this. Twisted everything his own way. Bewitched her. Fear that she'd—'Poor dear defenseless Wuggums your father has a monstrous uncaring inhuman side to him I never saw but we see it now don't we but we don't need him do we no now let me make it up to you

I TOLD HER THINGS I HAD NOT TOLD MY OWN BROTHER. WE BELONGED TO ONE ANOTHER. I FELT CHOSEN. WHO CHOSE HIM, PRAY? WHO GAVE INFORMED CONSENT TO EVERYTHING HITHERTO'S LOSS? I DESPISED HIM FOR FORCING ME TO HIDE THE FACT THAT I DESPISED HIM.

PAUSE FOR EPISODE OF DYSPNEA, VISUAL EVIDENCE OF ERYTHRURIA; R.N.'S LOCATION AND CLEARING OF PYURIC OBSTRUCTION IN URINARY CATHETER; GENITAL DISINFECTION; TECHNICIAN'S REATTACHMENT OF URINARY CATHETER AND GAUGE.

until I drop from bloody trying.' Missing something. 'Don't need him do we now there there.' Orbited him. Thought first and last. She had ceased to be the girl I'd—she was now The Mother, playing a part, a fairy story, emptying everything out to—. No, not true that it would have destroyed her, there was nothing left in her which would even have understood it, could so much as have *heard* the—she'd have cocked just so and looked at me without any comprehension whatever. It would have amounted to telling her the sun did not rise each day. He had made himself her world. *His* was the real lie. She believed *his* lie. She believed it: the sun rose and fell only—

[PAUSE for episode of dyspnea, visual evidence of erythruria; R.N.'s location and clearing of pyuric obstruction in urinary catheter; genital disinfection; technician's reattachment of urinary catheter and gauge]

THE FATHER: The crux. The rub. Omit all else. This is why. The great black enormous lie that I for some reason I alone seemed able to see through—through, as if in a nightmare.

[PAUSE for episode of severe dyspnea; R.N.'s application of tracheobronchial suction catheter, pulmonary wedge pressure;

technician (1)'s application of forcipital swabs; location and attempted removal of mucoidal obstruction in FATHER's trachea; technician (2)'s administration of nebulized adrenaline; pertussive expulsion of mucoidal mass; technician (2)'s removal of mass in authorized Medical Waste Receptacle; technician (1)'s reinsertion of O₂ feed into FATHER's nostril]

THE FATHER: Thrall. Listen. My son is evil. I know too well how this might sound, Father. *Te judice.* I am well beyond your judgment as you see. The word is *evil*. I do not exaggerate. He sucked something from her. Some discriminatory function. She lost her sense of humor, that was a clear sign I clung to. He cast some uncanny haze. Maddening to see through it and be unable—and not just her, Father, either. Everyone. Subtle at first but by oh shall we say middle school it was manifest: the wider world's bewitchment. No one seemed able to see him. Began then in blank shock at her side to endure the surreal enraptured soliloquies of instructors and headmasters, coaches and committees and deacons and even clergy which sent her into maternal raptures as I stood chewing my tongue in disbelief. It was as if they had all become his mother. She and they would enter into this complicity of bliss about my son as I beside her nodding with the careful, dutifully pleased expression I'd fashioned through years of practice, out of it as they went on. Then when we'd off to home and I would contrive some excuse and go sit alone in the den with my head in my hands. He seemed able to do it at will. Everyone around us. The great lie. He's taken in the bloody world. I do not exaggerate. You were not there to listen, drop-jawed: oh so brilliant, so sensitive, such discernment, precocity without vaunt, such a joy to know, so full of promise, such limitless gifts. On and on. Such an unqualified *asset*, such a *joy* to have on our roll, our team, our list, our staff, our dramaturgid panel, our minds. Such *limitless gifts* unquote. You cannot imagine the sensation of hearing that: *'gifts.'* As if freely given, as if not—had I even once had the backbone to seize one of them by the knot of his cravat and pull him to me and howl the truth in his face. Those glazed smiles. Thrall. If only I myself could have been taken in. My son. Oh and I did, prayed for it, pondered and sought, examined and studied him and prayed and sought without cease, praying to be taken in and bewitched and allow their scales to cover mine as well. I examined him from every angle. I sought diligently for what they all believed they saw,

A YOUTH WHOSE SOCIAL PERSONA WAS A BLANK AFFABILITY AND IN WHOM A READY WIT OR APPRECIATION FOR THE NUANCES OF ACCOMPLISHED ENGLISH PROSE WAS WHOLLY ABSENT.

natus ad glo—headmaster pulling us aside at that function to take us aside and breathe gin that this was the single finest and most promising student he'd seen in his tenure at middle school, behind him a tweedy defile of instructors bearing down and leaning in to—such a joy, every so often the job newly worthwhile with one such as—limitless gifts. The sustained

wince I'd molded into what appeared a grin while she with her hands clasped before her thanking them, thank—understand, I'd *read* with the boy. At length. I'd probed him. I'd sat trying to teach him sums. As he picked at his impetigo and stared vacantly at the page. I had circumspectly watched as he labored to read things and afterward searched him out thoroughly. I'd engaged him, examined, subtly and thoroughly and without prejudice. Please believe me. There was not one spark of brilliance in my son. I swear it. This was a child whose intellectual acme was a reasonable competence at sums acquired through endless grinding efforts at grasping the most elementary operations. Whose printed S's remained reversed until age eight despite—who pronounced 'epitome' as dactylic. A youth whose social persona was a blank affability and in whom a ready wit or appreciation for the nuances of accomplished English prose was wholly absent. No sin in that of course, a mediocre boy, ordinary—mediocrity is no sin. Nay but whence all this high estimate? What *gifts*? I went over his themes, every one, without fail, before they were passed in. I made it a policy to give my time. To this study of him. Willed myself to withhold prejudice. I lurked in doorways and watched. Even at university this was a boy for whom Sophocles' *Oresteia* was weeks of slack-jawed labor. I crept into doorways, alcoves, stacks. Observed him when no one's about. The *Oresteia* is not a difficult or inaccessible work. I searched without cease, in secret, for what they all seemed to see. And a *translation*. Weeks of grinding effort and not even Sophocles' Greek, some pablumesque adaptation, standing there unseen and appalled. Yet managed—he fooled them all. All of them, one great audience. Pulitzer indeed. Oh and all too well I know how this sounds; *te jude*, Father. But know the truth: I knew him, inside and out, and this was his one only true gift: this: a capacity for somehow *seeming* brilliant, *seeming* exceptional, precocious, gifted, *promising*. Yes to be *promising*, they all of them said it eventually, 'limitless *promise*,' for this was his gift, and do you see the dark art here, the genius for manipulating his audience? His gift was for somehow arousing admiration and raising everyone's estimate of him and everyone's expectations of him and so forcing you to pray for him to triumph and live up to and justify those expectations in order to spare not just her but everyone who had been duped into believing in his limitless promise the crushing disappointment of seeing the truth of his essential mediocrity. Do you see the perverse genius of this? The exquisite torment? Of forcing me to pray for his triumph? To desire the maintenance of his lie? And not for his sake but others'? Hers? This is brilliance of a certain very particular and perverse and despicable sort, yes? The Attics called one's particular gift or genius his *techno*. Was it *techno*? Odd for 'gift.' Do you decline it in the dative? That he draws all into his web this way, *limitless gifts*, expectations of brilliant success. They come thus not only to believe the lie but to depend upon it. Whole rows of them in evening dress rising, applauding the lie. My dutifully proud—wear a mask and your face grows to fit it. Avoid all mirrors as though—and no, worst, the black irony: now his wife and girls are bewitched this way now as well, you see. As his mother— the art he perfected upon her. I see it in their faces, the heartbreaking way they look at him, holding him whole in their eyes. Their perfect trusting innocent children's eyes, adoring. And he then in receipt, casually, passively, never—as if he actually *deserved* this sort of—as if it were the most natural thing in the world. Oh how I have longed to shout the truth and expose and break this spell he's cast over all who—this spell he's not even *aware* of, not even conscious of what he's about, what he so effortlessly casts over his—as if this sort of love were *due* him, itself of nature, inevitable as the sunrise, never a thought, never a moment's doubt that he deserves it all and more. The very thought of it chokes me. How many years he took from us. Our gift. Genitive, ablative, nominative—the accidence of 'gift.' He wept at her deathbed. Wept. Can you imagine? That he had the right to weep at her loss. That *he* had that right. I stood in abject shock beside him. His arrogance. And she in that bed suffering so. Her last conscious word—to him. *His* weeping. This was the closest I ever came. *Pervigilium*. To speaking it. The truth. Weeping, that soft slack face red and eyes squeezed tight like a child whose sweets are all gone, gobbled up, like some obscene pink—mouth open and lip wet and a snot-string hanging untended and his wife—*his* wife—lovely arm around, to comfort him, comforting *him, his* loss—imagine. That now even my loss, my shameless tears, the loss of the only— that even my grief must be usurped, without one thought, not once acknowledged, as if it were his right to weep. To weep for her. Who told him he had that right? Why was I alone undeluded? What had—what sins in my sad small life merited this curse, to see the truth and be impotent to speak it? What was I guilty of that this

should visit upon me? Why did no one ever ask? What acuity were they absent and I cursed with, to ask why was he born? oh why was he born? The truth would have killed her. To realize her own life had been given for—ceded to a lie. It would have killed her where she stood. I tried. Came close once or twice, once at his wed—not in me to do it. I searched within and it was not there. That certain sliver of steel one requires to do what must be done come what may. And she did die happy, believing the lie.

[PAUSE for technician's change of ileostomy pouch and skin barrier; examination of stoma; partial sponge bath]

THE FATHER: Oh but *he* knew. He knew. That behind my face I despised him. My son alone knew. He alone saw me. From those I loved I hid it—at what cost, what life and love sacrificed for the need to spare them all, hide the truth—but he alone saw through. I could not hide it from him whom I despised. That fluttered thrusting eye would fall upon me and read my hatred of the living lie I'd wrought and borne. That ghastly extrusive right eye divined the secret repulsion its own repulsiveness caused in me. Father, you see this irony. She herself was blind to me, lost. He alone saw that I alone saw him for what he was. Ours was a black intimacy forged around that secret knowledge, for I knew that he knew I knew, and he that I knew he knew I knew. The profundity of our shared knowledge and complicity in that knowledge flew between us—'*I know you*'; '*Yes and I you*'—a terrible voltage charged the air when—if we two were alone, out of her sight, which was rare; she rarely left us alone together. Sometimes—rarely—once—it was at his first girl's birth, as my wife was leaning over the bed embracing his and I behind her facing him and he made as if to hold the infant out to me, his eyes on me, holding my eyes whole with his and the truth arcing back and forth between us over the lolling head of that beautiful child as he held it out as if his to give, and I could not then refrain from letting escape the briefest flicker of acknowledgment of the truth with the twist of my mouth's right side, a dark little half-smile, '*I know what you are,*' which he met with that baggy half-smile of his own, what doubtless all in the room perceived as filial thanks for my smile and the blessing it appeared to imply and—do you now see why I loathed him? the ultimate insult? that he alone knew my heart, knew the truth, which from those I loved I died inside from hiding? A terrible charge, my hatred of him and his blithe delight at my secret pain oscillating between us and deforming the very air of any shared space

DO YOU NOW SEE WHY I LOATHED HIM? THE ULTIMATE INSULT? THAT HE ALONE KNEW MY HEART, KNEW THE TRUTH, WHICH FROM THOSE I LOVED I DIED INSIDE FROM HIDING?

commencing around shall we say just after his Confirmation, adolescence, when he stopped coughing and grew sleek. Though it's become ever worse as he's aged and consolidated his powers and more and more of the world has fallen under the—taken in.

[PAUSE]

THE FATHER: Rare that she left us alone in a room together, though. His mother. A reluctance. I'm convinced she did not know why. Some instinctive unease, intuition. She believed he and I loved one another in the strained stilted way of fathers and sons and that this was why we had so little to say to one another. She believed the love was unspoken and so intense that it made us awkward. Used gently to chide me in bed about what she called my 'awkwardness' with the boy. She rarely left a room, believed she had somehow to mediate between us, complete the strained circuit. Even when I taught him—taught him sums she contrived ways to sit at the table, to—she felt she had to protect us both. It broke—oh—broke my—oh oh bloody Christ please ring it the—

[PAUSE for technician's removal of ileostomy pouch and skin barrier; FATHER's evacuation of digestive gases; catheter suction of edemic particulates; moderate dysp-

nea; R.N. remarks re fatigue and recommends truncation of visit; FATHER's outburst at R.N., technician, Charge Nurse]

THE FATHER: That she died without knowing my heart. Without the entirety of union we had promised one another before God and Church and her parents and my mother and brother standing with me. Out of love. It was, Father. Our marriage a lie and she did not know, never knew I was so alone. That I slunk through our life in silence and alone. My decision, to spare her. Out of love. God how I loved her. Such silence. I was weak. Bloody awful, pathetic, tragic that weakn—for the truth might have brought her to me; I might somehow have shown him to her. His true gift, what he was really about. Slight chance, granted. Long odds. Never able. I was too weak to risk causing her pain, a pain which would have been on his behalf. She orbited him, I her. My hatred of him made me weak. I came to know myself: I am weak. Deficient. Disgusted now by my own deficiency. Pathetic specimen. No backbone. Nor has he a backbone either, none, but requires none, a new species, needn't stand: others support him. Ingenious weakness. World owes him love. His gift that the world somehow believes it as well. Why? Why does *he* pay no price for his weakness? Under what possible scheme is this just? Who gave him my life? By what fiat? Because and he will, he will come to me today, here, later. Pay his respects, press my hand, play his solicitous part. Fresh flowers, girls' construction-paper cards. Genius of him. Has not missed a day I've been here. Lying here. Only he and I know why. Bring them here to see me. Loving son the staff all say, lovely family, how lucky, so very much to be grateful. Blessings. Brings his girls, holds them up for me to see whole. Above the rails. Stem to stern. Ship to shore. He calls them his apples. He may be in transit this very— even as we speak. Fit diminutive. Apples. He devours people. Drains. Thank you for hearing this. Devoured my life and left me to my. I am loathsome, lying here. Good of you to listen. Charitable. Sister, I require a favor. I wish to try to—to find the strength. I am dying, I know it. One can feel it coming you know, know it's on its way. Oddly familiar the feeling. An old old friend come to pay his   I require a favor from you. I'll not say an indulgence. A boon. Listen. Soon he will come, and with him he will bring the delightful girl who married him and adores him and cocks her head when he delights her and adores him and weeps shamelessly at the sight of me here lying here in these webs of tubes, and the two girls he makes such a fault-less show of loving—*Apple of my eye*— and who adore him. Adore him. You see the lie lives on. If I am weak it will outlive me. We shall see whether I have the back-bone to cause the girl pain, who believes she does love him. To be judged a bad man. When I do. Bitter spiteful old man. I am weak enough to hope in part it's taken for delirium. This is how weak a man I am. That her loving me and choosing and marrying me and having her child by me might well have been her mis-take. I am dying, he impending, I have one more chance—the truth, to speak it aloud, to expose him, sunder the thrall, shift the scales, warn the innocents he's taken in. To sacrifice their opinion of me to the truth, out of love for those blame-less children. If you saw the way he looked at them, his little apples, with that eye, the smug triumph, the weak lid peeled back to expose the—never doubting he deserves this joy. Taking joy as his due no matter the. They will be here soon, standing here. Holding my hand as you are. What time is it? What time do you have? He is in transit even now, I feel it. He will look down again at me today on this bed, between these rails, entubed, incontinent, foul, wracked, struggling

AND HE WILL NOT EVEN KNOW HE EXULTS, HE IS THAT BLIND TO HIMSELF, HE HIMSELF BELIEVES THE LIE. THIS IS THE REAL AFFRONT. THIS IS HIS COUP DE THEATRE. THAT HE TOO IS TAKEN IN, THAT HE TOO BELIEVES HE LOVES ME.

himself, he himself believes the lie. This is the real affront. This is his *coup de theatre*. That he too is taken in, that he too believes he loves me, believes he loves. For him, too, I would do it. Say it. Break the spell he's cast over even himself. That is true evil, not even to *know* one is evil, no? Save his soul you could say. Perhaps. Had I the spine. Velleity. Could find the steel. Shall set one free, no? Is that not promised Father? For say unto you verily. Yes? Forgive me, for I. Sister, I wish to make my peace. To close the circuit. To deliver it into the room's air: that I know what he is. That he disgusts me and desp—repels me and that I despise him and that his birth was a blot, unbearable. Perhaps yes even yes to raise both arms as I—the black joke my now suffocating here as he must know he should have so long ago in that rocket I paid for without.

[PAUSE]

THE FATHER: God, Aeschylus. The *Oresteia*: Aeschylus. His doorway, picking at himself in translation. Aeschylus, not Sophocles. Pathetic.

[PAUSE]

THE FATHER: Nails on men are repellent. Keep them short and keep them clean. That is my motto.

even to breathe, and his face's intrinsic vacancy will again disguise to all eyes but mine the exultation in his eyes, both those eyes, seeing me like this. And he will not even know he exults, he is that blind to

[PAUSE for episode of ophthalmorrhagia; technician's swab/flush of dextrocular orbit; change of facial bandage]

THE FATHER: Now and now I have made it. My confession. To you merciful Sisters of Mercy. Not, not that I despised him. For if you knew him. If you saw what I saw you'd have smothered him with the pillow long ago believe me. My confession is that damnable weakness and misguided love send me to heaven without having spoken the truth. The forbidden truth. No one even says aloud that you are not to say it. *Te judice.* If only I could. Oh how I despise the loss of my strength! If you knew this hurt—how it—but do not weep. Weep not. Do not weep. Not for me. I do not deserve—why are you crying? Don't you dare pity me. What I need from—pity is not what I need from you. Not why. Far from—do stop it, don't want to see it. *Stop.*

YOU [cruelly]: But Father it's me. Your own son. All of us, standing here, loving you so.

THE FATHER: Father good and because I do I do do need something from you. Father, listen. It must not win. This evil. You are—you've heard the truth now. Good of you. Do this: hate him for me after I die. I beg you. Dying request. Pastoral service. Mercy. As you love truth, as God the—for I confess: I will say nothing. I know myself and it is too late. Not in me. Mere fantasy to think. For even now he is in transit, bearing gifts. His apples to hold out to me whole. Wishful thinking, to raise myself up Lazarus-like with vile and loathsome truth for all to—where is my bell? That they will gather about the bed and his weak eye will fall upon me in the midst of his wife's uxorious prattle. He will have a child in his arms. His eye will meet mine and his wet red wet labial lip curl invisibly in secret acknowledgment between he and I and I will try and try and fail to raise my arms and break the spell with my last breath, to depose—expose him, rebuke the evil he long ago used her to make me help him erect. Father *judicat orbis.* Never have I ever begged before. Down on one knee now for—do not forsake me. I beg you. Despise him for me. On my account. Promise you'll carry it. It must outlive all this. Of myself I am weak bear my burden save your servant *te judice* for thine is—not—

[PAUSE for severe dyspnea; sterilization and partial anesthesis of dextral orbit; Code for attending M.D.]

THE FATHER: Not consign me. Be my bell. Unworthy life for all thee. Beg. Not die in this appalling silence. This charged and pregnant vacuum all around. This wet and open sucking hole beneath that eye. That terrible eye impending. Such silence. 🦫

LENOX HILL

A G H A   S H A H I D   A L I

*(In Lenox Hill Hospital, after surgery, my mother—not fully
conscious—said the sirens sounded like the elephants of Mihiragula when his
men drove them off cliffs in the Pir Panjal Range.)*

The Hun so loved the cry, one falling elephant's,

he wished to hear it again. At dawn, my mother

heard, in her hospital-dream of elephants,

sirens wail through Manhattan like elephants

forced off Pir Panjal's rock cliffs in Kashmir:

the soldiers, so ruled, had rushed the elephants.

The greatest of all footprints is the elephant's,

said the Buddha. But not lifted from the universe,

those prints vanished forever into the universe,

though nomads still break news of those elephants

as if it were just yesterday the air spread the dye

("War's annals will fade into night / Ere their story die"), the punishing khaki whereby the world sees us die

out, mourning you, O massacred elephants!

Months later, in Amherst, she dreamt: she was, with dia-

monds, being stoned to death. I prayed: If she must die,

let it only be some dream. But there were times, Mother,

while you slept, that I prayed, "Saints let her die."

Not, I swear by you, that I wished you to die

but to save you as you were, young, in song in Kashmir,

and I, one festival, crowned Krishna by you, Kashmir

listening to my flute. You never let gods die.

Thus I swear, here and now, not to forgive the universe

that would let me get used to a universe

without you. She, she alone, was the universe

as she earned, like a galaxy, her right not to die,

defying the Merciful of the Universe,

Master of Disease, "in the circle of her traverse"

of drug-bound time. And where was the god of elephants,

plump with Fate, when tusk to tusk, the universe,

dyed green, became ivory? Then let the universe,

like Paradise, be considered a tomb. Mother,

they asked me, *So how's the writing?* I answered *My mother*

is my poem. What did they expect? For no verse

sufficed except the promise, fading, of Kashmir

and the cries that reached you from the cliffs of Kashmir

(across fifteen centuries) in the hospital. *Kashmir,*

she's dying! How her breathing drowns out the universe

as she sleeps in Amherst. Windows open on Kashmir:
There, the fragile wood-shrines—so far away—of Kashmir!
O Destroyer, let her return there, if just to die.
Save the right she gave its earth to cover her, Kashmir
has no rights. When the windows close on Kashmir,
I see the blizzard-fall of ghost-elephants.
I hold back—she couldn't bear it—one elephant's
story: his return (in a country far from Kashmir)
to the jungle where each year, on the day his mother
died, he touches with his trunk the bones of his mother.

"As you sit here by me, you're just like my mother,"
she tells me. I imagine her: a bride in Kashmir,
she's watching, at the Regal, her first film with Father.
If only I could gather you in my arms, Mother,
I'd save you—now my daughter—from God. The universe
opens its ledger. I write: How helpless was God's mother!
Each page is turned to enter grief's accounts. Mother,
I see a hand. *Tell me it's not God's.* Let it die.
I see it. It's filling with diamonds. Please let it die.
Are you somewhere alive, weeping for me, Mother?
Do you hear what I once held back: in one elephant's
cry, by his mother's bones, the cries of those elephants

that stunned the abyss? Ivory blots out the elephants.
I enter this: *The Belovéd leaves one behind to die.*
For compared to my grief for you, what are those of Kashmir,
and what are (I close the ledger) the griefs of the universe
when I remember you—beyond all accounting—O my mother?

UNLETTERED ELOQUENCE: THE LOST MAN'S RIVER TRILOGY

CHRISTOPHER MERRILL ON PETER MATTHIESSEN

The subject of Peter Matthiessen's epic trilogy, Edgar J. Watson, was said to have killed one person for every year of his life. At age fifty-five, the infamous Everglades outlaw was found with thirty-three bullets in his body. To this day no one will talk about it.

"The Watson story stuck in my mind like a burr," says Peter Matthiessen, recalling the genesis of his new novel, *Bone by Bone*. It was more than fifty years ago, on a boat trip with his father up the west coast of Florida, that he first heard about Edgar J. Watson. They were in the Ten Thousand Islands, a wild, unsettled tangle of mangrove forests, much of which lies in the Everglades National Park. Near the mouth of the Chatham River, his father remembered the story of a violent man who had either been executed by his neighbors or died in a shoot-out. Upriver was the Watson house (the only one in the park), where the pioneer staked his claim to a place in folklore—and now he belongs to literature. In *Bone by Bone*, the concluding installment of Matthiessen's *Lost Man's River* trilogy, which the author describes as an effort to feel his way into the truth of a complicated part of history, Watson tells his colorful story himself, correcting and expanding upon the local legend that, in the author's words, "had already turned into myth" by the time he started researching it, twenty years ago.

The Watson myth became an obsession for the globe-trotting writer. Although Matthiessen published a number of nonfiction books while working on the trilogy, including *Sand Rivers, In the Spirit of Crazy Horse, Indian Country, Men's Lives, Nine-Headed Dragon River: Zen Journals 1969-1982, Baikul: Sacred Sea of Siberia, African Silences*, and *East of Lo Monthang: In the Land of Mustang*, as well as a collection of short stories, *On the River Styx*, it was the complicated legacy of E. J. Watson, an entrepreneur and outlaw admired and feared alike by his neighbors, that filled his imagination. *Killing Mister Watson*, the first part of his trilogy was widely acclaimed when it appeared, in 1990; and when, in 1997, he published *Lost Man's River*, the longest of the three books, the epic scope of his project came clear. Here was an ambitious attempt to render the lawless world of the Florida Everglades through Watson, the only man arrested in the murder of the famous outlaw Belle Starr. But did he in fact shoot her during

Peter Matthiessen by Nancy Crampton

his sojourn in Oklahoma's Indian Territory? No one knows. Indeed, it was said that he killed fifty-five men, one for each year of his life, but the final tally (probably a handful) may never be known, partly because of the poverty of historical sources and partly because of the myths surrounding the man, some of which he himself fostered.

Matthiessen remains haunted by him. When we meet, in December, at his house in Sagaponack, Long Island, where he has lived for the last thirty-five years, he has just put the finishing touches on *Bone by Bone*. A tall man with a weathered face, dressed in blue jeans and a sweater, he bristles with leftover energy, unable to let go of what he calls his major literary work. But he is a born storyteller, and as he shows me around his property his ideas about his trilogy give way to recollections. Everything has a story: the immense piece of bone leaning against the front of his house is the crown of the skull of the fin-backed whale he found on the beach the day he completed *Men's Lives*, his celebrated account of the surfmen and baymen of Long Island's South Fork; lining the walking garden is a privet hedge—one of the last in the area; the outlying barn is now a Zendo, and Matthiessen, an ordained Zen priest, has been preparing his students to replace him. It is unseasonably warm on this bright Sunday morning, so he suggests a walk down to the beach.

Almost immediately we come upon a young equestrienne taking her horse through its paces, prompting Matthiessen to comment on the ways in which Sagaponack has changed. He was the only non-farmer in the area when he bought his property (the value of which tripled in the first year he owned it), and although he was, and always will be, considered "sum-

The demise of indigenous cultures, a common thread through Matthiessen's books, has played itself out on his home ground, too

mer people," the farmers took him into their gun club. He made good friends, educated his four children in one of the last little red schoolhouses in the Northeast, and witnessed both the crash of the potato industry and the spectacular land boom that radically altered the character of the town; as he writes in *Men's Lives*, since he moved in, "the selling off of the South Fork has become so frenzied that children of many local families, and the fishermen especially, can no longer afford to live where they were born." The flatlands beyond the cattails we pass are filling with the mansions of summer residents and weekend visitors— "city people," that is—and the largest house in America is under construction nearby. The demise of indigenous cultures, a common thread through Matthiessen's books, has played itself out on his home ground, too; hence the elegiac note in even the most ecstatic of his descriptive passages— in any setting.

"A friend pointed out that in my work there is always an elegiac pleading for us to wake up to the land and the rural people who give our country its character, its taste," he says. "That language is dying. Those insights are valuable. I never have been much interested in urban people, because first of all they're so well covered. Everybody writes about urban and suburban people. Very few deal with country people and the land. And the land is always a character in my books.

"I love the back country in Florida," he continues. "The coast, the inner part, the Glade, and all the ghost towns. I love the wildlife. And I was very interested in the Indian people, because they were the only people never defeated by the U.S. Army. They still had their language and customs. The Watson story was going to be a small element in the whole design, but it grew and grew until it took over like a strangler fig and killed the body of the supporting tree."

He made many journeys to the Everglades, writing for *Audubon* and other environmental journals, learning the countryside and customs of people he disagreed with on all manner of racial and political questions. Indeed he had to learn a whole new language in order to write the trilogy.

"I like local people," he says as we climb over the dunes and catch sight of the glittering sea. "They have a kind of

grit. They're laconic and funny. And they're in a tough spot. The government is trying to wipe them out to make room for tourists, and they're pissed off. Who can blame them? But you have to be able to speak their language before you can write it," he insists. "One reviewer of *Killing Mister Watson* said that I had shown the eloquence of the unlettered voice, and these people really are eloquent: their language is spare, their images stand up to the test of time."

They are also bitterly racist and insular. Ignorant, uneducated, under economic pressure as their livelihood, their way of life, is threatened, they blame outsiders, blacks, and Indians. "You have to see where they're coming from," Matthiessen explains. And he hopes that readers will view the trilogy as a denunciation of racism, the poison at the heart of the American experience.

The best storytellers take in the world—the confessions, anecdotes, and ideas of all sorts of men, women, and children; the diversity of flora and fauna; the inflections of the wind; the movement of the tides and stars; in short, the whole of nature—and then transform it into spellbinding narratives. Like Faulkner and Twain, Matthiessen has caught an essential American form of speech. In

Killing Mister Watson, ten different characters remember the pioneer, each in a distinctive voice. To wit:

> Life wasn't the same down in the Islands once all of them stories started up. His neighbors liked Ed Watson, sure, some called him "E.J." and was proud to let on to strangers what good friends they was with the man who killed Belle Starr. Well, their women never thought in that same way. To most of 'em, Ed Watson was a killer and a desperader who didn't draw the line at killing women, and them quiet, winning ways of his that women liked—that feller drew women like flies all the time we knew him—only made him the more dangerous to deal with. It was a long way to the next neighbor, too far to hear a rifle shot, let alone a cry for help. The men knew this but would not admit it. They liked ol' Ed—you couldn't *help* but like him!—but in their hearts, they was all deathly afraid.

This is only one version of him. Indeed, it may be argued that the trilogy is a grand divining effort to discover the complex truth not only about Watson but about the settling of America. It is a truth that Watson's own son, Lucius, the historian hero of the second novel, cannot learn, notwithstanding his decision to go live among the very men who shot his father—

a decision that haunted Matthiessen. But nothing in the historical record about Watson was true, and his other descendants offered the writer no help, because of the scandalous nature of his death: thirty-three bullets were removed from his body, and rumor had it the first man to shoot him was black.

"For a black man even to be in that group in 1910 is just extraordinary," Matthiessen says with a touch of awe. "How did this happen? Were they planning to kill him no matter when he came in on his boat that night, or was it in self-defense? They're still talking about it down there."

Who, then, was Watson?

"He's the Carnegie, the Ford, the Gould, the Rockefeller, but on a small scale, where he hasn't got the chance to do the real dirty work. He has exactly the same ambitions, and he'll kill to do it, like them. It's how the West was won, how our country was made. But no one said a thing about it if you were big enough—and that hasn't changed. Watson has vision, and he's very able, but he has a violent temper. He's always in trouble. In the last novel you'll find out why."

He learned more about him through the writing process, admitting that after he completed the first draft of the trilogy he still did not know him. His obsession helped: writing seven days a week, often until after midnight, he began to understand Watson, who was equally obsessed about carving out a place for himself and his family in the Florida frontier. And if the experience of writing at white heat for so long has left Matthiessen mentally exhausted, he hopes that an upcoming African safari will revitalize him; after all, he owes his publisher a book on cranes and one on the Siberian tiger. At the sight of a young man diving into the surf, he remembers coming here each year with the novelist James Salter for a ceremonial swim on November 1. Salter's wife would greet them afterward with a tray of martinis.

"And I'll tell you a dry martini as you come out of the surf in November is an experience you don't forget," he says with a laugh. "You could do it on a day like this."

Four loons and several gulls are swimming just offshore.

"There's bass right there—striper bass," he exclaims, pointing at the birds.

Writing seven days a week, often until after midnight, he began to understand Watson, who was equally obsessed about carving out a place for himself and his family in the Florida frontier.

"Good God, I wish I had a fly rod. I ought to go back and get one. We could jump in my truck and come here and see if we could catch some for lunch." He makes a mental note of our location on the beach, and soon we are on our way back to his house to gather fishing tackle. Before we begin to surf-cast, I ask how the descendants of the people he wrote about have responded to his work. Matthiessen replies with a story about returning to the Ten Thousand Islands on a book tour. He was invited to lunch at a local restaurant, and although most of the residents kept a cold, impeccable distance, three men came up to his table separately and said, "You the one who wrote the book?"

"I hemmed and hawed. And each of them said, 'Well, you told it like we heard it. That's what we heard from our dads and our granddads, and you got it right. You done your work.' They didn't say, 'We like the book' or 'We like you,' but 'you done your work.' They respected that. They could see their problems had been exposed. They felt their lives had been given some dignity."

Autumn Comes to Chicago

MICHAEL HAINEY

Spires looming.
Sky a soiled shroud.
Even when I was a kid
I knew this was my old country.
Where leaves get trapped
and battered in dark gangways.
Where cabbages boil in every kitchen
and bitter steam stains dim windows.
Where old Polacks sip Old Styles
in taverns on Ashland Avenue—
"Cold Piwo," those signs always say.
And outside, women, always women,
wait bundled for buses
grinding streets that reach to the horizon.

From my grandmother's attic, I could see
the garbage dumps beyond the railroad tracks.
They had been filled up years before I was born,
covered with new soil, sodded with fresh grass.
New land. And pipes were stuck here and there
spewing fire—"burning off the methane" they called it.
At night, I stared out the window
watching pale blue flames flicker like hopeful campfires of settlers on the prairie.

Yeh, these' stages

· JAMES KELMAN ·

IT DAWNED ON ME I HADNAY BEEN LISTENING TO MUSIC FOR
A LONG TIME. DAYS. QUITE A LOT OF DAYS. THAT WAS A SIGN
OF HOW THINGS HAD BEEN, MY PSYCHOLOGICAL STATE.

Not necessarily depressed. But maybe just out of things, on a sort of downside keel, no wind, just drifting about with the sails slack, not knowing fuck all, about what I was doing, not capable of thinking such thoughts. My partner had been gone for a while now and even going to bed was nothing to look forward to. I hadnt made the fucking thing since she left. The sheets and pillows disgusted me, the oily bit where my head lay. I wasnt washing properly, not one solitary shower in at least ten days. Falling apart! I saw myself in the typical male role, helpless without a woman, the poor wee boy syndrome. Yet this wasnay me. It was annoying to think I had let it go this far. Time to get a grip. I began in a straightforward way. I stuck on some music and let it blast out. I opened the curtains then the windows.

Then I was fuckt. I sat down on the edge of the bed and felt like killing myself. It got worse, I was into the kind of despair that makes suicide a positive move. I heard somebody chapping the door. Fuck them, whoever it was.

Which wasn't my real thought. At that moment my state of mind meant this sort of thought was beyond me. I just didnt budge, mentally or physically. I was staring at the floor, wondering about something to do with certain dods of oose and fluff, I think, if they might have been unusual insects, some uncharted species, it isnay as if science knows everything or has ever discovered everything. Even living organisms, some dont fucking even count; they arenay even worthy of being verified as extant, they arenay even worthy of reaching the state of the fucking dodo, an entry into an encyclopedia.

The chapping on the door, when it occurred to me that this indeed is what had happened; it took a bit of time to hit me. I wasnt capable of being there in the head at the same time the chapping was happening, I was behind the time the way it should be if you happen to be in an ordinary psychological condition, not well-being—who cares about well-being—but just an average sort of routine condition. There was a song I liked, I had been listening to, not recently, fairly recently, a couple of weeks, ten days, who knows—but it got to something, it was to do with it, the state I was in, the depth, that song was reaching down there, and it wasnt even the song it was the backing instrument, whatever the fuck it was, a box-accordion maybe, it was a depth, it was reaching some kind of depth, that way sunlight pierces right down through water, looking up and seeing it so far above, seaweed flowing by yer skalp. Needless to say by the time I opened the thing, the door, whoever it was had vanished, if somebody had been there, if at all. So this human absence there on the doorstep. I found I was scratching my bolls. I definitely needed to shower. Desperate. This human absence on the doorstep.

I tried to keep the train of thought going but didnay succeed. It was just overwhelming, the state I was in. Imagine being in such a state! Christ almighty. But at least I knew it was a stage. Or I thought I did. I hoped it was. I had that hope. I turned back and I didnt want to open my door, not any further, I was not wanting to go into the room, I wasnt wanting to. I was really scared.

But it wasnay a way to be, I knew that. Fucking hell man come on, come on, it's only yer woman's away for a few days, ye're not getting it the gether properly, that's all. I pushed open the door and saw it staring back at me, all these fucking bits and pieces; mainly they were hers,

I got sucked in, I could get sucked in, even now, even so, even yet

they belonged to her, but they were all out of place and topsy-turvy. Come on I said be practical be practical. And there was the television. It was a magnetic force, drawing my wrist, pulling me towards it, right into it, the other world, where my world was not, I got sucked in, I could get sucked in, even now, even so, even yet: just close yer eyes, keep yer way, tacking through the debris, the fucking wash, five stops and reach and ye shall find. So that made me smile, the syntax, then the sea, the fucking sea. I was seeing the stuff now, I stepped forward and picked up an empty can of lager. It was so easy. I just reached down

and lifted the fucker and squashed it, dumped it into a polybag that was lying there, I must have put it there for the purpose at some earlier time, an energetic instant. But I knew I had to watch myself and be attentive to these practical acts and not get sidetracked. There was the ashtray surrounded by ash and where was the hoover? but before that get the debris get the debris. And I replaced the bits and pieces, and then when I got into the kitchenette and saw the state of that! I just put in the stopper thing in the sink and piled in the dishes and the cutlery. Ran the tap, sprinkled the washing-up liquid. Saw the squeegee thing and started cleaning the floor, I wanted to sluice it. And all the empty ginger bottles, I stuffed them into another polybag. Absolutely no bother, I was well away. I was laughing to myself. Christ almighty man I knew it for sure, she was coming back, I knew she was coming back, maybe even that selfsame fucking afternoon, I knew it, I knew it for sure. Maybe she would even bring me a present. Christ, yeh, crazy, crazy.

Coming of Age

JOANNA GOODMAN

I. Ritual

The boy takes his turn inside the hut upheld by pillars *today shalt thou be with me*
in paradise and lies atop the girl faceup in the center *gather the fragments that remain* stolen
paroxysms of desire *that nothing be lost* between the props and pillars yielding the children's job
here is to stay afloat intractable for even Jesus went singing to the sacrifice *then shall they begin to*
say to the mountains: Fall on us; and to the hills, Cover us his father built this hut for them they are
the garden of delights the first and the last do not look up keep moving the pillars yielding *that*
nothing be lost crushed their flesh becomes word again each lovesick breath unseparating the
world *I am the voice of one crying in the wilderness* wild multitude arising *that they may also be one in*
us take eat *for this is the kingdom* domed above them the end of their desires yielding *wherefore*
unto this day the things seen are the things that *are*. This end is called *The Kingdom come*.

II. Hood River

We lie between two mountains—
brothers, T. told us, that legend says
fought so viciously over Mount Saint Helens
the Great One shoved a gorge between them.

A warbler on the new plum.

You say it could be an oriole or a goldfinch,

but I remember the poem for you anyway:

we hardened ourselves to live by. . .

Then a mole rippling the ground beneath us.

We drove 3000 miles with the windows shut.

Constructed our family trees, reconstructed,

somewhere between the Badlands and the Black Hills, your father,

disappearing now in a basement behind blinded doors.

Promise you won't let me suffer. Like that man.

The birds, meantime, gather on the wire,

twenty of them jerking their tight tufted heads side to side.

The eyes skinned of memory, does every second strike fully, as it happens?

How I wanted, west on 90, the sky spoon-feeding the Bozeman peaks,

to look at you long enough whatever veil

stops the moment from feeling real

would suddenly lift, the way the backwater,

too cold to stick a toe in, shuns us.

Your father ran seven years barefoot through the forest.

Chased and barefoot through the forest.

Stuffed to hide inside a haystack,

his mind all gone, he still bears the pitchfork marks.

I'll never meet him.

I'll never say, to you, I want to make it whole

to the afterlife, with you

I want to get there whole.

Kraków dnia 20. VIII. 193 r.

Za Wojewodę

Kierownik Oddz. Dróg.

WOJEWÓDZKI KRAKÓW

Opłata stemplowa skasowana na podaniu.

Dr Emanuel Stein

(własnoręczny podpis posiadacza pozwolenia)

The Polish ID card of Emmanuel Stein, the author's grandfather

REPARATIONS SPOKEN HERE?

RACHEL KADISH

The novelist journeys to Poland, the country her relatives were forced to flee in 1939, and finds that homelands can be hereditary.

This is how I thought it would be to travel in Poland: My image of myself, of my mother and the other family members I would meet there, was strangely irradiated. I pictured us as figures on a photographic negative—our dark hair white, our faces darkened, all of us staring with white eyes out onto a world that would not recognize us. On the sidewalks of Kraków we would weave mute and unseen, ghostly figures superimposed on a city oblivious to our presence.

I have yet to hear a discussion of Holocaust reparations that does not make me queasy. Terms like justice taste bitter; the money and property involved seem dangerous, inviting misinterpretation by those who would believe my great-aunts and others like them are just out for gain. Certainly the most important losses are irretrievable. At times I think of my mother's family as having been scattered at the detonation of an explosion. Even now, sixty years after the Holocaust and dispersed across several continents, we feel our windows rattle hard at the slightest tremor of anti-Semitism. *Rent*, my grandparents urged my parents when I was a child. *Don't buy.* The possibility of flight was a staple of my upbringing. Despite

On an outing, circa 1936. Second from right, in front and back rows, are the author's grandmother and grandfather.

my American passport and secure suburban childhood, I grew up knowing all I had could be swept away. Discovering as a child that I wanted to be a writer, I was irrationally uncomfortable to realize my career would be language-bound: What if I had to move to another country, another culture? Shouldn't I be developing skills more easily transplantable?

This trip to Poland was one I'd wanted to take all my life. And so when, a month before my twenty-ninth birthday, my mother and I coordinated travel plans with seven other relatives from Israel and England, when my relatives arranged July meetings with the Kraków-based lawyer handling the family's reparation claim, I refused to be deterred by what felt like a surreal scheduling coincidence: that very

week would cap off years of work. I had eight days to check over the galleys for my first novel. Resolved not to allow this obligation to eclipse the journey, I bundled up the neat uncut pages and a handful of red pencils; I packed my bag and boarded a plane to ground zero.

I had no intention of falling in love with Kraków, a city where more than sixty thousand Jews lived before World War II and where, as of the day I arrived, there remained only 150. I had no intention of falling in love with a single thing about Poland. I was there to see a world I'd heard about all my life, to keep my mother company, to see a building. Before the war my great-grandparents had owned a hotel in Krynica, a small spa town on what was then the Polish-Czechoslovakian border.

In 1939, when a small knot of my family members escaped to the east, the Germans were rumored to have made the hotel into barracks for Nazi soldiers. In 1949, at the start of the communist era, the Polish government turned the building into a high school. And in 1990, my great-aunts filed a claim on that property, as well as on the family's homes in Kraków: a claim that, by the time eight of us converged on Kraków this June, seemed to have been buffeted by every legal obstacle the Polish courts could muster.

There is a logic to setting obstacles in the path of reparations claims and one does not have to search hard for a motive. Most survivors are in their eighties and nineties; my youngest great-aunt just turned seventy-five. My mother, raised by refugee parents in New York City, speaks the Polish of a five-year-old: the age at which she learned English. In a few years, there will be no one left who cares enough to do the legwork involved in pursuing the claim—no one left who ever spent a night in a room of the hotel, no one left who can decipher the legalistic Polish of the necessary documents. It seems abundantly clear that the Poles are waiting for my relatives, their memories, their fluency in Polish, to die.

The moment we boarded the plane, I asked my mother to teach me Polish. I knew the trip would be hard on her; she'd never been to her parents' homeland, though they had raised her on a diet of Polish history and European sensibilities. Not one known member of my family remains among the aging Jews of Poland: those who failed to escape to the east in 1939 did not survive. I would be the youngest of our group: the "third-generation survivor," as someone would label me, jarringly, that week. The oldest, at eighty-four, had not been back to Poland since before the war. *Jeden, dwa, trzy, cztery.* By the time we landed I'd learned to count to four; my pronunciation, as I'd hoped, kept my mother laughing. I rubber-banded the galleys—I'd made some progress on the plane—and together we stepped into the airport.

I had no intention of falling in love with Poland, but this is what happened when my mother and I reached Kraków. Boisterous Israeli relatives greeted us at the

I had no intention of falling in love with Poland, but this is what happened when my mother and I reached Kraków

terminal. They led us into the wide streets of the city. And here, in this country that I'd never visited, I turned every corner to find a familiar scene. "This is where your grandfather grew up," an aunt would tell me, and I would think: Yes, I knew the building would be on that side of the street. Homelands, I quickly discovered, can be hereditary. Through story upon story of my grandparents' vanished world, the blueprint of this city had been inscribed in my mind.

The feeling was so strong it took me by surprise: we belonged here.

While two of my relatives met with the reparations lawyer, the rest of us explored the city. The degree of déjà vu was unsettling. Everywhere we went, every window, every doorway of the old Jewish neighborhood seemed to represent a long-ago cousin or schoolmate. At dinner that first night, I sat with my assembled family and listened to conversations that ricocheted between Polish, English, and Hebrew, often within one sentence. To say we weren't mute is an understatement. One aunt chatted with her son in Tel Aviv via cellular phone; another stretched over a fleet of dinner plates to check whether the flowers on the table's centerpiece were real. My mother accidentally answered a Polish waiter's query in Hebrew and then, stumbling in a Polish dredged from childhood, requested ice cream rather than ice in her water. Everyone laughed. My relatives had never seemed so colorful, so individual.

The feeling was so strong it took me by surprise: *we belonged here.*

For three days, I was part of a vibrant Jewish family in Kraków. For three seductive, merciful days, Kraków was ours. Felek, my grandmother's high school boyfriend, now eighty-five, took us to a centuries-old café and sat us at the same corner table where he and my grandmother broke up one afternoon in the 1930s. "I was young. I was not good to her." Tears gathered in Felek's eyes as he described their argument, decades before my grandmother's illness and death. "She cried so hard I didn't know what to do." He walked us by the club where they used to dance every Tuesday afternoon. ("The usual dances. Foxtrot. Tango.") We sat in outdoor cafés on streets lined with pastel-colored buildings. We walked along the river, admired the Wawel castle. Sipping soda alone one morning at an umbrella-shaded table, I felt a hand on my shoulder.

Felek, in the square for a business meeting, had spotted me. There is little for which one feels more grateful than to be recognized in a strange city.

Without a heartbeat's hesitation, I chose to let it happen. Shedding the armor of prescience with which we approach pre-Holocaust Europe, I allowed the thought: If I forget about the anti-Semitism, I can feel at home here. Knowingly—eagerly, even—I dropped the leaden weight of caution and boarded a train that I knew could only lead to betrayal. I let myself be enchanted by the city. It was an act of love for my grandparents, both Polish patriots in their youth, neither of whom had lived to make this family trip. History is patronizing toward those who lived it; I chose, for these few days, to ignore history and see Poland through their youthful eyes.

My Israeli relatives shopped; my mother and I attended a concert. We visited my grandmother's high school. Waiting for the tour to begin at the university where my grandfather fought anti-Semitic regulations, I sat on stone steps and continued work on the galleys. I looked at the pages

For once I didn't feel the need to apologize for being serious, for caring about something out of synch with my own generation.

in my hands, and for the first time ever I did not feel privately like a freak for writing this novel, set in modern Israel but narrated in part by a Polish Holocaust survivor. For once I didn't feel the need to apologize for being serious, for caring about something out of synch with my own generation. I wasn't drawn to this material because I was somehow morbid, but rather because this place, its politics and priorities and sensibilities, had been alive for me for as long as I could remember. Here, in a country I never expected to feel like home, I recognized myself.

We admired the woodwork of a famous church altar, videotaped the trumpet player at the top of the Mariacki Church. Mapping out an extinct family life, we visited those Kraków homes my great-aunts are trying to reclaim, and those that were so badly trashed when the Nazis crammed hundreds of families into this section of the city (the ghetto depicted in *Schindler's List* and which is now low-rent housing) that my aunts have chosen not to claim them. We photographed stairwells, graffiti, a rusted motorcycle covered by a tarp. Dirty kittens poked their heads out of

Dumpsters, dogs barked from balconies as we approached. The buildings' residents looked on with folded arms.

Certain kinds of love exact a price. It wasn't until a loud noise sent me jumping or tears surprised me during a cab ride that I had any indication of the stress beneath the surface of those days. A celebratory gun salute at a parade in Kraków's main square sent hundreds of pigeons wheeling into the air. As the beating of wings subsided I watched them settle on rooftops and wondered, heart still racing, how high the birds flew in the 1940s.

By now I knew a few Polish phrases, enough to construct a sentence here and there. I made increasingly bold forays into the language. "*Ja nie jestem kapusta!*" I am not a cabbage. By now I could count to six. If I kept this up, I realized one afternoon—if I kept this up, and the aged kept dying—I'd be able to count the remaining Jews of Kraków.

On the last night before the Israeli and British contingents of my family departed, we sat for hours over dinner. Felek serenaded one of my Polish relatives in German: *I still remember that day. . . . when*

> *The rest of us watched rapt, as if their reunion in this city of their youth were a holy rite.*

the player piano played. . . . that was when you first said you loved me. The two of them ordered vodka, then beer. They hunkered down at the end of the table, speaking Polish. The rest of us watched rapt, as if their reunion in this city of their youth were a holy rite.

And then my relatives were gone. For half a week I'd lived a rich Jewish family life in a Kraków that no longer existed, an invisible city as tempting and ephemeral as one of Calvino's. Now silences felt haunted. I practiced counting to ten. There were 149 Jews left in Kraków. One had died. The square was full of pigeons.

Things did not look good for my great-aunts' claim, according to the lawyer. Another few months and he would know more. Maybe.

The countryside en route to the Tatra Mountains was so picturesque it felt absurd. The next day my mother and I were to leave Poland; now, after a week in the city, we passed white goats and spotted cows on green grass, old men on bicycles. We passed round haystacks, rolling hills, people hand-raking hay in the fields. Even the puddles along the train tracks had ducks in them.

It took all morning to reach Krynica, a small, pretty town in the foothills of the Tatra Mountains. We made our way down streets lined with arched lampposts and tourist shops.

My great-grandparents' hotel was an imposing, run-down gray building. The broken outdoor basketball hoop and the graffiti announced the high school's long tenancy as clearly as the signs over the offices that had been my family's private rooms. You could see that it had once been beautiful. Small balconies dotted the side of the building.

It would be easy to speak of my great-grandparents' hotel as being of symbolic value to my family; after all, it has been decades since any of us resided in Poland or frequented the Tatra Mountains. But I think of a symbol as something that takes up residence in the mind. When I stood outside my great-grandparents' hotel, the building's impact was visceral. This was the place where my grandmother and great-aunts vacationed; where my great-grandmother, whom I knew, presided over the family in her ultradignified fashion, switching into various Romance languages lest the maids be eavesdropping. In this town my grandmother swam and hiked her way into her twenties, when she defied convention and went to law school; here she skied, reluctantly, with a suitor eleven years her senior. That suitor broke a leg on the slope, and my grandmother took care of him in the hotel while he recovered. To my older relatives, the hotel is home: the inheritance their parents wanted them to

The author's grandmother and three great aunts with their governess. Kraków, 1917.

have. To me it is the place where my grandparents fell in love. I wanted to see it, touch the curtains, look out at the world through those windows.

A man stepped out of a door, stared at us for a moment, then—with what seemed to be a warning look—stepped back inside.

We circled the property, took pictures. Passersby slowed to watch us. By this time we knew the routine.

But as we stood in front of the building, something unexpected happened. Normally my mother is the one to push ahead; I am the nervous nelly, the voice of caution. Yet now I told my mother I wanted to try to go into the building. And my mother, as though sensing some nameless threat, did not want to budge. I don't know if I've ever seen her so meek.

I can't say whether it was some wordless threat radiating from the ground that stopped us, or whether we feared some actual violence from those in the building. I can only say that it happened

To me it is the place where my grandparents fell in love. I wanted to see it, touch the curtains, look out at the world through those windows.

as swiftly as a blow: our personalities, our individual quirks, were swept away. Under the watchful eyes of strangers, we were no longer Anna and Rachel, granddaughter and great-granddaughter of David and Miriam Herzig. We were simply Jews, one and two generations removed from catastrophe. And so we responded as if reading from a script, taking on our roles with astonishing ease. My mother, born on the run to refugee parents, suddenly knew to tread carefully. A small, helpless gesture of her hands was her only explanation: *I can't* or *I'm afraid*. And I, American-born, was sharply aware of one emotion: I was furious. I had a right to be here, and believed, for just a moment, that nothing in this damn country could intimidate me. For that instant, before common sense asserted itself, I was angry enough for two—because I was an American and could afford to be.

I didn't push her to approach the building's custodians. And much as I chafed to march in and declare myself at home, I knew no combination of Polish words likely to elicit help from the strangers holding the keys to this building. I knew, too, that my grandparents and great-grandparents, with lifetimes' vocabularies at their fingertips, had received little sympathy from their countrymen. I stood on the cracked pavement, armed with little but a smattering of numbers: evidence of all I could not express. My mother, her own vocabulary as useless as mine, stood mute beside me.

It was a sunny afternoon, an unpopular time for travel; on the Kraków-bound train the compartment, meant for six, was empty. For hours we might have been the train's only passengers. My mother and I took turns reading aloud, checking galleys against original manuscript, page after page. In our alternating voices the words sounded reassuring. Then we stopped; I continued scanning the pages by myself. The silence was eerie, interrupted only by the rhythmic thumping of the tracks.

During that train ride I stumbled, numb and exhausted, across the first way of thinking about reparations that made sense to me. The words before me were a tender language, a language for those willing to listen. But in a country where people have been reduced to artifacts, ashes, statistics—where our words are ignored or silenced and those who have benefitted from the murder of the Jews maintain a thick denial—only a more strident language penetrates. Reparation is a vocabulary of its own, each transaction a crude syllable sounding into a void.

Where all else fails, it forces hearing on those who would rather be deaf. On that train ride I still didn't know what to feel about the political consequences of reparations, or the moral complexities. I didn't know, either, that my family's reparations claim would continue to be deadlocked, that the ensuing months of effort would produce nothing but frustration. I knew only that, for the first time ever, I was not ambivalent about the reason to pursue my family's claim. I wanted my great-aunts heard.

I tried to quell the irrational notion that my mother and I were the only two passengers on a driverless train. I tried to focus on the pages in front of me. So it was my mother who saw the graffiti painted on a barrel by the railroad tracks: *Juden Raus*. "Jews Out." I looked up in time to see only freight cars: windowless bolted metal, heavy barred doors. In the picture my mother took as we passed through that anonymous country train yard, a brown hulking car fills the frame of the camera. Faintly superimposed on it is the ghostly image of a young woman—plaintive, pale, shocked Jewish features. Even now it takes me a moment to recognize my own face, reflected in the window of our compartment as my mother released the camera's shutter.

Two Poems
— *by* —
Philip Fried

Fur Piece

This weasel is ours, body and soul,
locked in a closet until, glassy-
eyed, it is suddenly produced to dazzle,

drunk with the notion of a night
on the town, dazed with anticipation,
sleek with perfume that flows from mother.

Obedient to the need for glamour,
it leaps on her back, benign vampire,
pretending to gnaw at her lapel.

(The only blood it sucks is illusion.)
The smirk and sinews have been worked
back into its amiable body

and care has been taken to make this forest
creature fit for the wilderness
of lurid horns and brassy neon.

Riding shoulder-high to theaters,
where it glassily inspects the actors,
or soaks up song like a richer perfume,

then off again, gliding with high-steppers.
Then ducking into a subway hole
after a night of smug parading.

Those nights are over and now the family
that used to be waits in the dark closet
with the shoe trees and the sly weasel,

frozen unless a path goes deeper—
into the coats—through the gut of a moth—
to a lichen wing. And he can lead them . . .

Indian Summer at Spring Lake

Ocean, close but invisible, stills
the village except for this worrying
halyard twanging the flagpole's mast
that might be the mast of an empty

craft, at anchor, riding the swells.
They razed everything
to build here, the rambling Victorian
houses too big—the grass

clipped. Last night in my one-night room
my father came back in a dream,
saying, "You don't need to be blue,"
dapperly dressed in a three-

piece suit, but he got seedy as
the dream wore on, needing
a shave. His words were suddenly trailing
off, with news from nowhere

I can't remember. Like the living,
the dead confuse the deepest
wisdom with gossip, scarcely knowing
where one begins or the other

ends. A door like the sideways lid
to a music box has opened
on the melody of teaspooned laughter
at breakfast. A refugee

from summer, this bee is searching for last
sweetness. A bougainvillea
in a pot that hangs from the porch is crazily,
gradually spinning—awry

arms, too many, embracing nothing.
A boy could cycle forever
down this well-mannered avenue,
saluted by telephone poles.

This body, standing hand on saddle,
might start. He points to the endless
end and his gesture goes all the way
at first. The bougainvillea

tries every way at once.

THE HOURS, BY MICHAEL CUNNINGHAM

ANGELICA GARNETT

How does one read a novel objectively if one is a character in it? The niece of Virginia Woolf enters the world of Michael Cunningham's Woolf-oriented novel The Hours, *and finds a heady mix of reality and fiction.*

When, about a fortnight ago, I received a letter from Amy Bartlett, whom I had met only once on a recent visit to New York, asking me to write about *The Hours*, by Michael Cunningham, an author I had never heard of, I was both intrigued and surprised. Her letter was perfectly clear, but I did not immediately understand why she had thought of me, as I do not usually review books, and I only knew what she had briefly told me about *Tin House* magazine. It was not until I had read the first two pages of the book that realization dawned. Here I was, reading a description of my aunt's suicide, described as though the author had been on the spot at the time. It became clear that I was to be dragged back into the past—a past I had so often tried to avoid or escape (but had also struggled with). Not only was I to be made to confront the fact that I was unavoidably Virginia Woolf's niece (something that can, on occasion, resemble a superb feather in my hat), but I was

Virginia Woolf with Angelica Bell, 1939, by Lettice Ramsey, courtesy of Mrs. Jane Burch

mond during the First World War, at a time when Virginia is beginning to think of her subsequent novel, *Mrs. Dalloway*. The second theme concerns a modern Clarissa, nicknamed Mrs. Dalloway, living in the New York of the 1990s. She is about to give a party for an old friend who has just won an important prize for his poetry. The third theme, emotionally the least close to Virginia Woolf's writing, is concerned with Laura Brown, a young mother and housewife in California after the Second World War,

expected to do far, far more than this—to forget that I was her niece and to read the book for its own sake, as though in fact I were someone else.

The Hours—a title analogous to Virginia Woolf's *The Years*—is a beautifully written novel that does, in fact, play with time, reserving a surprise for us towards the end that, like the narrowing of a shutter lens, seems to bring everything into focus. Three disparate yet connected themes are woven together. First, Mr. Cunningham imagines the daily life of Virginia and Leonard Woolf in their house in Rich-

who is a possible extension of Mrs. Brown, a character invented by Virginia in her essay, *Mr. Bennett and Mrs. Brown*, that considers the plight of women writers in her own day. Intellectually representative of Virginia's *situation* as a writer, Laura has things to say that, because of her sex, are never listened to.

As I continued to read I was seized by an immense reluctance. A hedge of resistance rose immediately around me. Why should I have to go through all the pain of breaking through it, and for whom? Perhaps the most cogent answer lies in the fact that I am Virginia's niece, that willingly or not, I have inherited her instinct to rise to a challenge.

I decided to read the book and write about it at the same time—to provide a sort of running commentary, a crablike approach that expresses both reluctance and fascination. No doubt, like the child I was at Charleston and in Mecklenburgh Square, I shall in the end be caught and held up to confront some sort of truth—though whether it will be that of my grandfather Leslie Stephen (editor of the *Dictionary of National Biography*), objective and historical, or that of Virginia, dedicated to the impression of the moment, I do not know.

Whether I am objective or the reverse, I cannot forget that until her death, I knew Virginia intimately, seeing her once, perhaps twice a week. When, as so often, she often came to a tête-à-tête tea with my mother, Vanessa Bell, I would catch a glimpse of what such an intimate sisterly relationship could mean. Having no sister myself, this was my only way of knowing how ineluctably close, how delicious and yet how devastating,

Whether I am objective or the reverse, I cannot forget that until her death, I knew Virginia intimately, seeing her once, perhaps twice a week.

was such a God-given fact of life. They understood each other at the drop of an eyelid, the movement of a finger. Words, Virginia's prerogative, were, between them, unnecessary—and Vanessa had few to give. Nevertheless they gossiped, mostly about old and half-forgotten relations, cultivated by Virginia for the rather chilly sake of pure amusement. She kept them going, as she might have kept flowers alive in a glass of water, adding a drop every now and then. Vanessa did not enjoy this much, being only too glad that now, because she lived in Gordon Square rather than Kensington, these creatures, as she would have called them, no longer turned up on her doorstep. But for me the gossip was fun. Sitting on the floor cutting out paper dolls with a pair of blunt scissors, I enjoyed it all thoroughly, while learning my aunt by heart. And years later, half grown-up, I would visit her alone in Rodmell and she, like an eagle on her nest, would bend down, with curved beak nudging and gently pushing, encouraging me, as often as not, to write—in her view, an art that was highly superior to painting.

I knew Virginia—but not as one adult knows another. I was without guile, without prejudice, and without insight, and, since she was not my mother, without too many expectations of her. She was for me both an event and a shadowy pillar, taken for granted like the bowl of fruit on the table or the light coming through the window—not always there, but all the same a constant element in family life, an echo of Vanessa, although without her power or certainty. She was, therefore, like another child, much easier to get on with. She was a possible confidante, a fellow conspirator (the only one I had), a repository for my secrets: did she know, I would ask, that I preferred Mrs. Ede, the daily help, to Lottie the cook, or that cart horses loved sugar? The result of this confidence was that in Mecklenburgh Square, when I went there to tea, we spent hours throwing sugar lumps out of the window to the patient cart horses far below in the street. And if greater secrets there were, in spite of her terrible reputation for untrustworthiness, she nobly kept them.

She spared me, of course. To me she never talked of her headaches or her anguishes, but then I doubt if she did much to anyone, although in her relationship with Leonard they could not be overlooked. But Leonard made the mistake of assuming that the doctors were right, that milk in the morning and refusing her permission to write when she felt like it would help. Early nights did, no doubt, have some effect. But the gulf of misunderstanding revealed by the insistence that she eat more, which Mr. Cunningham touches on, still appalls me. How could it have helped? How was it that no one had more insight? Even though I understand Leonard's anxiety, his constant preoccupation with the inherent dangers, it is difficult to accept the unwillingness of his mind to see further. He cannot be blamed, but he cannot be entirely exonerated either. How close they seemed when they came to tea—and yet what a desert must have lain between them—a desert that, in the last months of Virginia's life, must have seemed to her like the Sahara and the Gobi rolled into one, uncrossable and as dry as a bone. The water of the Ouse probably seemed heavenly by comparison.

I knew Virginia— but not as one adult knows another. I was without guile, without prejudice.

On page 4 of *The Hours*, we are shown Virginia standing on the riverbank as her mind goes back to Leonard. She sees him with a beard, and my mind leaps to the defensive. This was something he never had, never could have had (except perhaps in Ceylon?). I continue reading, as prickly as a hedgehog, progressing through what I must admit are luminous streams of the chapters Mrs. Dalloway and Mrs. Brown, characters appropriated it seems by Mr. Cunningham. I do not yet understand. Then when I reach page 113, there is the shock of encountering the character "Angelica." We are *en famille*, in the Woolf's garden at Hogarth House during the First World War in a very convincing scene when Quentin has found a dying bird in the street. And Vanessa says, "But this is the bird's time to die, we can't change that." True, Vanessa has a formidable reputation for truthfulness—but I can't hear her saying that. It is too modern an attitude, too keen on educating, implying the conscious desire not to hide death from the children—and in my memory, at least, Vanessa was not interested in teaching. Virginia's reaction to this is convincing, typical and likely, but wrong. She thinks: "Vanessa does not harm her children but she does not lie to them either, not even for mercy's sake." I find myself reacting strongly to this, since what else did Vanessa do to me, for the first seventeen years of my life, in failing to tell me that Duncan Grant was my father, not Clive Bell? When she eventually did tell me, it must have been a strange and upsetting experience for her, since as far as I remember I hardly reacted at all. She must have told Virginia of it, but what she said I do not know. Their relationship was strange—Vanessa condemned to be the eldest, the surrogate mother—to feel as though she was not appreciated for what she really was. But then when Vanessa was in trouble, Virginia's facade, constructed presumably in self-defense, evaporated, and she tended to Vanessa's needs with a sensitivity, a depth of understanding that, when Virginia in turn needed the same from Vanessa, was not forthcoming. For each the view of the other was distorted.

As Virginia's niece, I find myself being put into the book so convincingly that I have to remind myself that the situation never actually occurred, that I never went to Hogarth House for the simple reason that I had not yet been born. At the back of the book all the other surviving members of the family are thanked—but although my name has been used—together with those of both my brothers, now dead—I am omitted from this list. Here I am reading about "myself," feeling at the same time as though, for Mr. Cunningham, I did not exist! Such a feeling would have been familiar at times to Virginia.

Now it is time for me to cut down the hedge and step outside into the world of Mr. Cunningham. So I actually do and succeed in seeing everything, for the moment, quite differently.

I leaf back to the first chapter and find in it a power that is, even seen through my distress, considerable. Once more I see Virginia's descent to the river, her irresistible intention. Is this what suicide is? How was it in reality? Can I dare to think of it so directly, so factually? Does Michael Cunningham teach me how to do so? The scene as he imagines it seems to me plausible—though a trifle too conscious and aware. Perhaps his sensitivity makes this inevitable. How can anyone know? Here I am more hampered than he, since, because it was a real event in my life, I have not his detachment or freedom to imagine. And at the time, which I well remember, what did we feel—what did I feel? *Nothing*, it seemed, since my feelings were embryonic, laid over by those of others, by the fear that Vanessa's feelings might overcome her entirely. I did not and

still do not know what I "really" felt, being at the time twenty-one and in love— my life beginning against a background of war, bombing, devastation, even possible invasion. Like everyone else, I had, of course, no idea of what war might mean. But it was there, incipient, threatening, swallowing up ordinary, delightfully ordinary daily life. It was this that, with Virginia's death, went out of the window. And another reality that suddenly descended with Clive's voice on the village telephone, telling me she had disappeared and was feared dead, although as yet no one knew anything for certain. I rode home on my bicycle to tell my lover and eventual husband David/Bunny. He was— I now see him—at the top of the stairs, standing against the light. But having heard my inept and broken phrases, he descended, holding out his warm protective arms. No doubt he understood more than I did and took it, or most of it, on his broad shoulders, which, although it prevented me from feeling for myself, was what I wanted. So I bicycled over to Charleston, seven miles away, to find Vanessa and Duncan, who had just returned from London, in the kitchen, where we embraced— what else was there to do?—a trio suddenly soldered together, awkward but close. We all knew what it meant: the end of the world as it had been, the era of youth and joy. Nothing like Virginia would ever happen again.

The echo of her suicide would remain with us for the rest of our lives, becoming for me, at least, more and not less real, even perhaps—who knows? —influencing my eldest daughter to commit the same act thirty years later.

People have the right to choose; that is what is so difficult to remember, just as they have the right to ask for help. Virginia in her own way did ask—but no one knew how to help—which is where we too shared her sense of failure.

That was why Leonard, the color of ashes, was sitting on the drawing room sofa at Charleston, telling Nessa the facts, the sequence of events, as far as he knew them. He was now alone—totally alone, after thirty years of marriage and companionship that had been as close as one of those strange animal relationships one hears of occasionally—perhaps that of a tiger living with an eagle—unable to fly, and now bound inexorably to his own lone path through the jungle. He was trembling with shock, emaciated, noble and, above all, dependable.

And so, I say to myself, what has Michael Cunningham to do with all this? What has his own path been? What has brought him to write this book? Obviously he is in love with Virginia—so much is evident. It is obvious too that he is a gifted writer and a subtle thinker and that I, perhaps, am not equal to analyzing his deeper purpose.

Now, this morning, I have finished the book. It is now, if ever, that I should be objective. But this is both impossible and even undesirable. I have been confusing objectivity with the *idée reçue*, with opinions that belonged to an older generation and had been chewed over 101 times already—ideas that might be found in the *Dictionary of National Biography* or *The Times*, and might safely be uttered at the dinner table without fear of being mis- understood. "Good," "bad," "remarkable," and "second-rate" were the words these cultural arbiters used, that even Leonard, with his half-hidden passion, would have listened to with respect and that very probably my grandfather Leslie would have accepted without question. They would have found it hard to agree that such judgments, apparently irrefutable, were as subjective as anything else. It was this tendency that Virginia fought against, that she was inspired to dislodge with her sensibility, her feeling that such a way of looking at life was disgracefully superficial. It was in fact the Achilles' heel of Blooms- bury—the attempt to find reasons, to stay in the arid upper levels of the brain, refusing to watch and wait for deeper revelations. But the dangers of a more intuitive approach are great. Sensibilities may fail and imitation creep in.

It was in fact the Achilles' heel of Bloomsbury— the attempt to find reasons, to stay in the arid upper levels of the brain, refusing to watch and wait for deeper revelations.

At which end of the spectrum does Mr. Cunningham lie? At least this much can be said, that he has achieved something singular in that his work is both original—that is, something that very few other writers would even wish to do—and something that, at moments when I feel most like Virginia's niece, I am tempted to call pastiche. He has so identified himself with her that, on every page, the reader hears her voice. Every character in the book is in one way or another, a part of Virginia. They impersonate her fictitious characters, while being at the same time an invention of Mr. Cunningham's, belonging to our own present day world. Or their thoughts are hers, or might, convincingly, have been. This amounts to a tour de force that is impressive in its intelligence and single-mindedness, and is also, at certain moments, moving.

But for me these moments are precisely those in which Virginia's part is least. For example, Mr. Cunningham's characterization of Mrs. Brown, and the delicate, perceptive description of her relationship with her little boy Ritchie—these seemed, at first reading, perfectly done, true and without any false touches. They are not, in spite of Mrs. Brown's inhibited desire to commit suicide, typical of Virginia's style of writing or thinking. One knows of course that this is as it should be. As Virginia herself said in her essay, "Mrs. Brown" can be impersonated not only by the "clean and threadbare old lady" in the railway train, but by anyone the author chooses to invent, since she is "life itself."

There is immense sensibility, immense wisdom in this book, immense delicacy— and no sentimentality, which is what makes me think it is the product of a rare mind. Mr. Cunningham seems in this instance to be a chameleon, and, as all such must be, is infinitely, almost photographically sensitive, sharing this quality with Virginia Woolf herself.

Angelica Garnett
6th November 1998
Forcalquier, France

THE RESURRECTIONIST

RICHARD McCANN

A transplant patient grapples with the psychic complications of receiving a donated liver.

HERE IS WHAT HAPPENED:

I was cut apart.

The liver of a dead person was placed inside me so I might live again. This took twelve hours and thirty-three units of blood.

But who was I afterward?

I could still recall the body I'd had when I was ten, the body in which I carried what I called "myself," walking along the C&O Railroad tracks or crossing the divided highway that separated our house from the woods; a heavy, modest body, dressed in husky-size jeans from Monkey Ward and a brown corduroy car coat that my mother chose, identical to those my uncles wore back in the mining towns they lived in. I could recall the body I'd had, nervous and tentative, when I first made love at seventeen. But these bodies were gone, as was the body into which I'd been born, these bodies I'd called "mine" without hesitation, intact and separate and entire.

Three months after my liver transplant I flew to Nashville to visit my mother in the nursing home. She sat in a blue housecoat at a folding card table, slowly spooning a Dixie cup of ice cream to her mouth. "Marie, your son's here," the nurse kept telling her. But my mother wouldn't look up except to look through me. She'd begun her own metamorphosis since the last time I'd seen her, withdrawing into the form of a bony old woman who only sometimes recognized my brother or me.

"Is this your son Richard?" the nurse asked, a grade-school teacher prompting a forgetful pupil. My mother shook her head: no, no.

At night I sat at her bedside. "I'm here," I whispered as she slept. "I made it through. I'm here."

I didn't know if she could hear me. For a

> At night I sat at her bed-side. "I'm here," I whispered as she slept. "I made it through. I'm here."

while I tried to work on the letter of gratitude I was planning to send to the strangers the transplant coordinator referred to as my "donor family," though I knew nothing about them or their loved one whose liver I'd received. I couldn't figure what to write to them that would seem neither too rehearsed nor too intimate, though I planned to repeat some remarks I'd heard in a support group meeting, thanking them for "the gift of life" and assuring them that the highest form of giving occurred, as theirs had, when neither the donor nor the recipient was known to one another.

For a moment my mother shifted beneath her blanket, murmuring in her sleep. I put down the pencil and closed my eyes. *In just a second*, I thought, *she'll say my name*.

"Mother," I said, though she said nothing further. I wanted us back as we had been, restored to what I felt were our real and original bodies, my mother smoking a cigarette on the stoop of our old house in Silver Spring and me beside her with a bottle of Pepsi in my hand, though I knew if my mother were able to ask what had happened to the liver I was born with—the one she'd given me, I sometimes imagined, for it had once been a part of her as well as of me—I could have told her only what the surgeon had told me: "It was sent to pathology and burned."

I flew home the next morning. On the plane I noticed the man beside me staring as one by one I swallowed the half-dozen immunosuppressants that kept my body from rejecting the organ it would forever perceive as foreign, and for a moment I felt my own sudden strangeness, even to myself, as if I were a distinct biological phenomenon, constructed in a manner different from that of my fellow passengers hurtling though space in a pressurized cabin, drinking coffee and reading their magazines.

"I'm a liver transplant recipient," I told my seatmate.

He wanted to know if my new liver was male or female or white or black.

I said I didn't know; he said that if it were him he'd sure want to find out.

But I didn't, or at least I didn't think so, and I was relieved when the plane began its descent. Somewhere over the Alleghenies my seatmate had asked if I'd heard about a man with AIDS who'd gotten a liver from a baboon.

No, I hadn't.

No one dared the obvious: the mother was the mother of a child who was dead, even if his lungs were still drawing breath on earth.

But in my transplant support group I had heard of recipients who'd waived their rights to anonymity to arrange what they sometimes called "reunions," inviting their donor families over for *yahrzeit* rituals and barbecues, and I'd heard of donor families who'd secured the names of recipients, showing up unannounced on their doorsteps, bearing bouquets of mixed flowers and brightly colored mylar balloons.

"Maybe it's kind of like discovering you're adopted or finding your birth mother," one woman said, confiding to our support group her anxious plans for meeting the mother of the teenage boy whose lungs she'd received.

No one dared the obvious: the mother was the mother of a child who was dead, even if his lungs were still drawing breath on earth.

Sometimes I too fantasized that I had an alternate family that was eager to receive me as flesh and blood, especially as my mother retreated farther and farther into a world from which I was excluded, as when she imagined that I was her dead brother and called me by his name. But my fantasies of a happy meeting with a donor family were vague and unspecific, even less concrete than the fantasies I'd concocted as a child, waiting for George Maharis from Route 66 to pull up to the house in his Corvette, ready to speed me away to what I felt sure was my real future.

My fantasies of a painful meeting, however, were explicit and detailed with dread. What would I say if my donor family were to ask to place their hands on my belly so they could feel the liver softly pulsing within?

How could I refuse them? I owed these people everything. I was alive because of a decision they'd made while standing in the bright fluorescence of a hospital corridor. Wasn't the liver more theirs than mine?

I imagined myself hesitating when they reached to touch me, and I imagined them demanding of me, with what I would have agreed was a rightful anger, "Who do you think you are?"

We are made of the dust of old stars, our grade-school teacher told us; we are made of leaves and sediment and the mulch of life. But I was made also of something rescued from the graveyard, I realized after the transplant, and if I was now among the resurrected, I was also the resurrectionist—the name given in the nineteenth century to the grave robbers who sold corpses for dissection to physicians and anatomists, trafficking in bodies and parts.

I don't recall when I began to think of what is medically called "the non-heart-beating cadaver donor" as neither a noble but faceless benefactor nor as a nonhuman organ source, ...

I don't recall when I began to think of what is medically called "the non-heart-beating cadaver donor" as neither a noble but faceless benefactor nor as a nonhuman organ source, but rather as someone particular and separate who'd lived his own life before he died. I don't recall when I began to think of a donor organ as a bearer of its own set of cellular memories and not just as some sort of bloodied and perishable apparatus that one could airlift a great distance in an Igloo cooler marked HUMAN HEART or HUMAN EYES. In the eleven months I spent waiting for a transplant, I could barely acknowledge what was happening to my own body as my liver rapidly failed: abdomen grossly distended from accumulated fluids; muscle wasting as my body cannibalized itself for nutrients and proteins; pale stools streaked with bile; profound and constant exhaustion; brief spells of aphasia; cramps and sudden hemorrhages, blood puddling in my mouth from ruptured esophageal varices; skin the color of copper and eyes the color of urine.

I do recall a spring afternoon a month before my transplant, when I was lying on the grass in Rock Creek Park, back from the transplant clinic where I'd overheard a nurse telling someone in the next room—I couldn't see who—that a high number of teenage donors die not from car wrecks but from suicide.

I didn't want to know this, not as I myself was growing so desperate for a donor. As soon as I left the clinic, I asked a taxi driver to take me to Rock Creek Park—"Are you all right?" he kept asking, afraid of my appearance—where I'd often gone when I was well to sunbathe with my friends, though now I was alone. I paid the fare; then I was lying on the unmowed grass, attempting to lose myself in the song I could hear playing on a far-off radio, pretending that my whole life consisted of just one word: *sunny, sunny.* . . .

But it didn't work. My donor had begun to claim me, or so it seemed; I felt as if he'd somehow been constructing himself inside me without my knowledge as I was dying, though he was still alive and waiting for nothing unforeseen. Perhaps he's here right now in this park, I thought, or perhaps he's in another part of the city, crossing a street against traffic or standing at a pay phone or waiting for the bus that will bear him home from work. For a moment it seemed as if there were but the two of us left in the world, me and my blood brother, though one of us would soon be dying.

Don't die, I wanted to whisper, though I didn't know if I was speaking to him or myself.

I suppose I found out four weeks later: the hospital paged me past midnight to say they'd located a suitable donor.

. . . but rather as someone particular and separate who'd lived his own life before he died.

My friend Sarah drove me to the E.R. The whole way I kept checking and rechecking the contents of the small suitcase I'd packed six months before—silk dressing gown, twenty-dollar bill, packet of Dentyne, razor and toothbrush and comb; I couldn't stop touching these things, as if they were all that was left holding me to earth.

I knew what would happen when we got to the hospital— X ray, EKG, and enema; introduction of IV lines, one in the left hand and another beneath the collarbone, for sedatives and cyclosporine and antibiotics. For months, I'd been trying to prepare myself for the transplant surgery, studying the booklets the doctor had given me, one with drawings of abdomens marked with dotted lines to represent incision sites, and another with a diagram showing how a pump-driven external system of plastic tubing would route my blood outside my body during the time when I would have no liver.

I was prepared to wake in the ICU, as in fact I did, unable to speak or move, brain buzzing like high voltage from prednisone.

I was prepared to wake in the ICU, as in fact I did, unable to speak or move, brain buzzing like high voltage from prednisone.

But I was not prepared for what came the week after that: the impact of the realization that I had participated in the pain and violence and grief of a human death. *You have to face what you've done*, I kept telling myself as, each day, I watched myself in the mirror, growing healthier, until even my jaundiced eyes were white again: I had taken a liver from a brain-dead corpse that had been maintained on a ventilator during the removal of its organs, so that it looked like a regular surgical patient, prepped and draped, with an anesthesiologist standing by its head to monitor blood pressure and maintain homeostasis, its chest visibly rising and falling with regulated breath.

"It's not like you killed him," my friends kept telling me.

"I know, I know," I said to quiet them, though I didn't know, not really. But I did know, as perhaps my friends did not, that it isn't just children who believe they can kill with the power of a thought or a word. After all, I had sat in the clinic waiting room with other transplant candidates, joking that we should take a rifle up to the roof to shoot some people whose organs we might like. "I wish we'd been at the

Texas Book Depository with Oswald," one man had said.

At night in bed I often thought of the person who'd died; when I was quiet, I could feel myself quietly grieving him, just as I was grieving my own body, so deeply wounded and cut apart, though still alive.

"I'm sorry," I wanted to tell him.

Sometimes I woke in the middle of the night, troubled to realize that I had taken a piece of him inside me, as if I had eaten him to stay alive. When this happened I often forced myself to think of it longer, though I didn't want to, as if I were a member of a tribe I'd read about a long time before in an old ethnographic text that described how the bereaved dripped the bodily fluids of the dead into their rice, which they then made themselves eat as an act of reverence and love.

In this state, I could not console myself. I got up and sat on the sofa. *So here I am*, I thought, *right on the edge of the unspeakable. . . .*

Other nights I thought of the donor with a great tenderness, sometimes perceiving him as male and sometimes as female. These nights, I placed my hand over what seemed to be still her liver, not mine, and slowly massaged the right side of my body—a broken reliquary with a piece of flesh inside—all the way from my hip to

the bottom of my rib cage. "It's okay, it's okay," I whispered over and over, as if I were attempting to quiet a troubled spirit not my own.

If I could, I would undo what I have done, I thought, though I knew that if I had to, I would do it again.

I wasn't new to survivor guilt. After all, I'd been living for a long time in the midst of the AIDS epidemic while so many of my close friends died: Larry, Ed, Darnell, Allen, Ricardo, Paul, George, Arcadio, Jaime, Wally, Billy, Victor, and David.

In this sense, it had been a relief to be diagnosed, to have a progressive disease that threatened my life, to be bivouacked with the others. "It's like you're one of us now," my friend Kenny had told me. "It's like you've got AIDS."

But I couldn't tell him it wasn't true, at least not after the transplant; it wasn't the same at all. I'd outlived everyone, even myself.

What did Lazarus want after he stumbled from the cave, tied hand and foot with graveclothes, his face bound about with a napkin? *Loose him*, Jesus said, and *Let him go.*

I survived. It's two years since the transplant. Here I am, in my new life.

I want to unfurl.

I want to become my gratitude.

I want to fly around the world.

I want to be a man with a suntan. The man in the Arrow shirt.

And above all, this: I want to complete what I've written here—these fragments, these sticky residues of trauma—by adding just one more line before the words THE END: "It's a miracle."

It is a miracle, of course. I know that. Just the other day, for instance, stopping at a sidewalk fruit stand and buying a blood orange: *Oh*, I thought, *this will replace the blood I lost.* I carried the orange to the park, where I sat in the sun, lazily devouring its juicy flesh, its piercing wine-red tartness. *There's nothing more than this I need*, I thought. *I'm alive. I'm alive.*

But what happens after the miracle? What happens after the blinding light of change withdraws and the things of the earth resume their shadows?

What happened to Lazarus after his resurrection? On this, the Gospel According to St. John is silent. Did Lazarus speak after he was commanded from the grave and his shroud was loosed? Did he thank the One who was his Savior and then walk back into the house with his sisters Mary and Martha so they could wash him clean? Or did he turn in anger toward his Savior, demanding to know why He had tarried so long with His Apostles before coming? *If thou hadst been here, I had not died.*

Where did he go afterward? Did he live a long life? Did he forget his time in the grave?

Here is where I went after my resurrection: Miami Beach, Sarasota, Raleigh, Nashville, Peterborough, Madrid, Barcelona, New York City, and Provincetown.

And I went back as an inpatient to the hospital—five more times, at least to date. The hepatitis goes on, the doctor tells me. The transplant doesn't cure it. It gives the virus a new liver to infect and feast upon. (*Dear donor, forgive me, I can't save your life. . . .*)

A year after the transplant, just after the

Did Lazarus speak after he was commanded from the grave and his shroud was loosed? Did he thank the One who was his Savior and then walk back into the house with his sisters Mary and Martha so they could wash him clean? . . .

anniversary the social worker called my "first birthday," these things happened: low-grade fever; weight gain; edema; jaundice; sudden and unwanted elevations in alkaline phosphatase, bilirubin, and liver enzymes. *This can't be happening*, I thought, *not again*.

"We need to biopsy the liver," the doctor said. He said we needed to measure the progression of the disease by assessing the extent of new cirrhotic scarring. I knew what that meant: it meant the story wasn't over, as I so badly wanted it to be. It meant that things were uncertain.

"Don't worry," the doctor said as he sorted through my file. "We can always discuss retransplantation."

No, I thought, I can't hear that word, not ever again, especially if it's applied to me. Where was the miracle now? I was supposed to have been restored. I was supposed to have been made whole. I wanted to loose the graveclothes; I wanted to unbind the napkin from my face; I wanted to be through with death forever.

Instead I was sitting in a windowless medical office, waiting for the phlebotomist to come and draw more blood. I wasn't sure I had the heart for more miracles.

Did Lazarus believe he was done with death after his resurrection? There's no record of whether Christ cured him of the sickness that had killed him in the first place, before he rose again; there's no record of the pain his body must have felt after having lain four days in its grave— long enough to have begun to decompose and (as the Gospel says) *to stinketh*.

As for me: For three weeks I got worse, then I slowly got better. A few months later the doctor said there'd be no need to discuss retransplantation, at least not yet, at least not in the immediate future.

It wasn't a miracle that pulled me back, at least not then. I was saved not by a sudden and divine intervention but by the persistent and real efforts of physicians, some with Cartier watches and others wearing scuffed shoes. The story didn't end with a tongue of flame or a blinding light. Each morning and evening

... Or did he turn in anger toward his Savior, demanding to know why He had tarried so long with His Apostles before coming?

I monitor myself for organ rejection, as I'll do for the rest of my life: blood pressure, temperature, weight. I go to the clinic for blood draws; I await faxes detailing test results.

Here is what happens after the resurrection:

Your body hurts, because it's hard to come to life again after lying so long in a grave, but you set goals and you labor to meet them, holding yourself up with your IV pole as you shuffle down the hospital corridor, slowly building back your strength. You learn your medications; you learn to pack your wounds with sterile gauze; you learn to piss into a bottle and shit into a pan. It's work, preparing yourself for sunlight.

Then the day comes when you are allowed to wash your hair and shower. A little while later you're walking down a street.

People you've not seen in ages stop to ask how you're doing; you say you're doing fine, you're doing great. It's life again, dear ordinary life! Life as you hungered for it, with its pleasures and its requirements.

Yes, it's life again, your life, but it's not the same, not quite. Or so it seems, because you can't forget how it felt to lie in the close darkness of that grave; you can't forget the acrid smell of the earth or the stink of the moldering graveclothes, especially now that you know, as you never did before, that you're headed back to the grave again, as is everyone, and you know this with a clarity you cherish and despise.

The gift of life is saturated with the gift of death.

Sometimes, sleepless at night, I imagine I'm back in the hospital the night of my transplant, lying naked in a cubicle behind a thin curtain, waiting for a nurse to prep me for surgery. *This is how it feels to lie in a cold room*, I tell myself, because this might be my last night on earth and I want to feel everything, to feel once more how life feels, each breath in and each breath out.

The nurse comes in and instructs me to lie on my side. She administers an enema. *This is how it feels to be filled with warm water*. I go to the toilet and afterwards I look at myself for a moment in the bathroom mirror. When I return to the cubicle and lie down, the nurse says she must shave the hair from my abdomen, all the way from my groin to my chest. "I hope my hands are warm enough," she says, spreading the shaving soap across my stomach. She touches the cold razor to my belly, and I think, *This is how it feels to be alive.*

TWO POEMS
by
ALEŠ DEBELJAK

Translated by Christopher Merrill

· · · · · · ·

Woman's Shadow

What you implanted in my marrow I translate into a language
I haven't mastered yet: the cadence of a scream reaching
into the heart, the rumbling of an underground train, church
naves without altars, gods murmuring in the pelvis. You:

you rose from a shell like a delicate sculpture from the furnace
of a glass-blower. You taught me anguish and humility
before the gospel of a demanding prophet. And the freedom
of a doe bounding across the meadows of a slumbering heaven.

I can't reach them without you. I hear the chestnuts crackling
on the terraces of my village. The asphalt is cooling. I don't care.
I'd rather tremble with delight, like a house on the verge of restoration,

when you sing a new melody. At the darkest hour of the day you show me
the alphabet of wind and fate and seeds. I read stains in history's cellar.
I know my home will be there, where you mark off the wild garden.

Homecoming

A crust of thin ice cracks and signposts change. Summer snow
slides down the Karavanke mountains. Pale princely faces. Blood
will soon return to their cheeks. The frozen woodpecker's knock
against the windowpanes awakens us. Early morning. Light teems

from cracks in the earth. What a melancholy odor rises from the boots
exhausted by the deep marsh! Above the roofs, winds from the west and south
mix, and blindness ends on the threshold of the grave. Now all of us who
left home at birth gather at this holy hour. No one needs the broken

eggshell. From its pieces emerges the map of a country which defies
oblivion. In the square, the tank trap is again at a standstill. An old woman
lovingly raises her arms free of desire and fear. The mystery of ten days

is over. She awaits them peacefully, recognizing the despair under their helmets.
They think she is their mother comforting them. The face of a soldier
old as a Celtic vase drowns in the murmuring water that might fill the dry well.

TROUBLEMAKER

by
Christina
Chiu

"HEAR ME, ERIC?" MA SAYS, TURNING FROM THE TV. SHE'S GOT HER SWOLLEN FEET PROPPED ON THE RIM OF THE TUB, WHICH SITS DEAD CENTER IN THE MIDDLE OF THE KITCHEN.

"I don't want to hear any more complaints from Lao Gong. Twice this month already. Pretty soon he's going to speak to the landlord." Ma's got on a new uniform. She's done up her hair with a thick red ribbon and she's even got lipstick on, too. It's New Year's. Big tips tonight, she says.

"Damn cripple," I say, crossing the imaginary line into my room. "The only ba-la-lang going on around here's in Lao Gong's ugly fat head."

"Ai." Ma sighs, giving me a look like she's sucking on a pickled plum. She shakes out her apron. "He's old."

"Relax, Mrs. Tsui," Billy says, blowing a bubble with his gum. "We're just going to hang. I gotta go help at the store later any-

way." We toss our knapsacks on the top bunk and dump ourselves below on my brother Johnnie's. The Asshole would shit if he saw us here.

I give Billy a look like, Wish she'd get lost already. With my foot, I snap the skateboard up and catch it in my hands. The wheels spin, its ball bearings clicking in the air. The hallway leading to the door's got my name all over it: Skate, go ahead, skate, it tells me. There's a scuff mark from the ollie over the tub; a turned-around S from pretending to thrash a halfpipe.

On TV, Oprah blabs on about all that feel-good garbage Ma likes to hear. "Everyone says they want to be happy,"

Oprah says. "But when asked, they don't have an image of what that really means to them." Ma nods and mumbles in agreement. She uses her arms to push herself up, then irons the apron. She does this slowly, pressing her weight onto every wrinkle, even the ruffles at the bottom. There's a crescent-shaped burn the size of a nail clipping. The thing is clean, scrubbed by hand every night in the bathroom sink, but against the new outfit, I realize it isn't white the way it should be. Closer, maybe, to dust balls, and as ratty as a dishrag. Ma folds it in half, then half again, and irons it to get square creases into it. Like that's going to make it look like new?

An hour before the Asshole gets home, I think. Just enough time to get down that flip kick over the tub.

"You're going to be late, Ma," I say.

She checks the clock on the wall. "Ai. Have to hurry." She ties the apron around her waist and pulls on a jacket. It's too thin by itself; she has to wear a coat over it. Billy and me, we hang on Johnnie's bunk. The thing smells like him. Stale greasy B.O.

Ma heads out the door. She has a way of walking like a spider. Quick and soundless.

Skate, go ahead and skate, the hallway calls.

I drop to my knees, dig out the ramp from under the bed, and just to be sure she's gone for good, race to the window. The red ribbon disappears toward Canal. Billy and I move all the food to the kitchen counter, fold the table, and snake the shower curtain up over the metal rod. I set the ramp against the tub, find some speedmetal on the radio, and skate to the end of the hall.

"This is the shit," Billy says.

With my back against the door, I focus on the space above the rim of the tub and picture myself there: just me and board and air. "Yes," I say, pumping my back foot. Just as I close in on the tub, I kick back, and boom!—*flying*. My stomach flips. Nothing can pull me down.

"Yeah, man. Shred it up!" Billy says.

Lao Gong bangs his cane again. "Damn cripple," I say.

Billy races to the end of the hall. "Check this out," he says. "Totally bionic." But the front door opens and in walks Johnnie. Billy stops mid-step, his sneaker squeaking against the floor. Lao Gong bangs away at his ceiling.

"What the—didn't Ma say to cut that out?" The Asshole moves toward me until I've got my back against the wall. I can smell the grease in his clothes. He tries to stare me down.

"Get out of my face," I say.

"What was that?"

I take a swing but miss, and he catches me in a headlock. I try to wrestle him to the ground, but his hold tightens and tightens and I start to choke. Billy's face is like, "Oh, fuck." Johnnie dumps me

a bunch of six-packs. The sky seems lower than yesterday, like one of these days it'll fall and we'll be lost inside it. There's the crackling sound of firecrackers. Once in a while, a rocket. Nothing much.

Billy checks out the scene below. "Man, I never knew your brother got so uptight."

"Fucker can't get laid."

I HOPE YOU DIE, I THINK.
I HOPE THAT GIRL DUMPS

into the tub. My head bangs against the spout and my knees catch the porcelain edge. I cough and spit, cough and spit.

"Get up," he says.

I hope you die, I think. I hope that girl dumps your sorry ass and then you die. Billy's still got that frozen look on his face. Spit hangs from my mouth. I start to laugh.

"What's so funny, ah?" Johnnie asks.

I wipe the drool with my arm. "Nothing."

Johnnie jerks his arm, making me flinch. A snarl curls the side of his lip. "Didn't think so."

The Asshole tells us to get lost and we do. First to McDonald's for a couple of Big Macs and fries. Then to the roof where one of the guys from school set us up with

The wind cuts through my jacket and, like a blade, forces its way through me. I kick a flowerpot and a bony dead plant topples over. The new bump over my ear throbs, and I imagine all the ways a chick could dis the Asshole. I gulp my beer. His girl could take off with some other Asshole, tonight. Yep. Take off with some Hong Kong kid who owns a Porsche.

Wind sweeps over the rooftops and funnels down through the street, lifting a crumpled napkin into the air. People squeeze slowly past one another. Somewhere in the dark, firecrackers snap like pistols. Smoke rises and drifts. It smells crisp and sour.

"We need a bunch of those," I say.

"Nah, what we *need* are a bunch of

bottle rockets. Remember Jimmy Ho? Heard he lit one of those, then threw a stuffed mannequin off the roof. Everyone went nuts."

I crush the beer can between my palms. "Idiot, I was there."

"You were in on that?"

"Sewed the gloves on myself."

"Shit, did that thing really knock some guy unconscious?"

YOU ON YOUR SORRY ASS AND YOU DIE.

"Nah. That's Jimmy's big mouth. The thing dropped on a truck. But it was still awesome. You should've seen their faces. Everyone ran—thought someone got shot."

"He got the cell for *that*? Ain't shit."

Just then, Johnnie steps out of the building. A bow tie pokes over the top of his coat. His hair's slicked back shiny like a mat, and not even the wind can get to it. He's got one of those Asian parties tonight. Tavern on the Green, he said, like he's some kind of rich-ass. Like he's one of those yuppies with a job on Wall Street.

"He going to score or what?" Billy asks.

"With that rich-bitch girlfriend he's got? *Right*. One look at this place and she'll be

making a b-line back to Westchester."

"You seen her?"

"Nah. Just listen to the shit he talks on the phone." I squash the aluminum can between my palms. The cold metal sticks to my skin. I could peg the Asshole right now and he wouldn't know what hit him. As if he read my thoughts, Johnnie looks back and gives me the finger. My elbow flinches.

"Do it," Billy says.

I shove the can into my pocket. "Nah, too easy."

"Right. Like you would have gotten him? You couldn't peg me right here, your arm sucks so bad." Billy chucks a can behind a heap of empty flowerpots. This gets me laughing. Billy eggs everyone on like this.

"Shut up," I say.

A cop appears on the other side of the street. He glances up, and just like that, Billy and I are eating gravel. My beer spills. "Did he see?" I ask.

Billy snorts and breaks out the Chinaman rap he uses at the store. "Wew-come China-tong. Want buy watchie? Gucci only ten dolla."

The wind cuts down the neck of my

jacket. "Ten dollars?" I add. "Oh, my. So expensive? How about nine?"

"Nine-la, okay-la. And a happy fucking new year to you, too, bitch."

Finally, we down our last beers. That's when Lao Gong appears. He clutches the rail in one hand, the crutch in the other. He's got on the same gray coat he wears all the time. Even from up here, I get that sour, old-man stink.

"What's *he* up to?" Billy mutters.

"Got me. He never leaves the place."

Billy crushes a can. It folds together like an accordion. "Your chance, man. Get him good."

"Shut up."

"What? Scared?"

"I said shut up."

"Ten bucks says you are."

The guy drags one leg, then the other, down the steps. Couldn't miss even if I tried, I think. With a flick of the wrist, the can whirls through the air. At first, it seems as though it'll arc past him. But one, two, three and tock! The thing smacks his ear. A sound that's tinny and flat.

Lao Gong freezes. His fingers splay apart. The cane falls, the handle knocking, knocking, knocking against the cement. There's a sharp whine before the old man crumbles.

"Oh, shit," Billy says, doing a hyena laugh. The old man drops, knocks into a passerby, then hits the pavement. People scatter. A black cloth slipper tumbles into the street.

"Bionic, man!" Billy says.

We nose-dive onto the roof before anyone sees us.

I put out my hand. "Ten bucks."

The ambulance catches our attention. The siren squeals, red lights flickering on and off, on and off. The old guy's still on the sidewalk. He's lying on his side, one leg twisted at a funny angle. The wind flaps a lonely strand of hair. Some white guy crouches next to him and takes his pulse.

"He's dead," Billy says.

"No way. Wasn't any beer in the thing."

The medics move around the body, checking the pulse at his wrist. They lift his eyelids. Too much white stares up at us.

"Get up, old man," I whisper. "Get up."

A crowd circles as they put him on a stretcher. Cops appear. We junk the beer and scramble downstairs. The roof door shuts out the screaming horns, and for a second, it's dark and quiet.

In the apartment, the lights are out.

There's the lamplight from the street. Billy's got the door, and me, I'm by the window. The ambulance takes Lao Gong up Mott, and the red lights swirl down the street until they turn onto Canal. At first, people move around the space, but as the siren goes muffled, the crowd presses in until it's gone.

Where's the slipper? I wonder.

The cops get to the neighbor's door within the hour. "Mr. Lee no home," Mrs. Lee says. The chain rattles against the door frame.

"May we ask a couple of questions?"

"No home. Mr. Lee no home." The door bangs shut.

Feet appear like black shadows beneath the door to our apartment. One, two, three solid, even knocks. Billy looks at me like, *Shit.*

The cop raps again. One, two, three; one, two, three. We don't answer; they don't move. They know we're here, I think. Everything stops. It's Jimmy Ho who jumps into my head: "That first night, thought I'd shit my pants," he'd said. Sweat drips down my neck into my jacket. Billy starts to whisper to himself. I'm like, Shut up, already. He's praying. The guy doesn't even go to church, and he's praying.

The feet finally step away from the door

. The boards creak under their weight.

"Shit," Billy mutters. "Oh, man."

Neither of us says another word until the cops are gone.

Outside, the street's beginning to empty out. Wind funnels through Mott, making a low flute sound. A napkin circles on the pavement. Johnnie appears, head tucked low into his coat, walking straight into the wind. I knew the sucker wouldn't score.

Just as Johnnie enters the building, the cops appear. The officer's voice is low and muffled, but I can hear Johnnie slurring, "Yes, officer . . . no, officer." Johnnie lights a cigarette, then adds, "Jesus, who'd be sick enough to do a thing like that?"

Just like that, I know that he knows.

"Gotta take off," I tell Billy, grabbing my board. "Asshole's back."

Billy blocks the door. "Got fried brain in the head or something? Can't go out there."

Then it's too late. A key twists and Johnnie's there, a shadow with the fluorescent light behind him. Smoke funnels from his nostrils.

The light clicks on. Before I can even see straight, Johnnie's got me in a headlock.

"Billy, if I were you, I'd take off," Johnnie orders, and just like that, Billy's gone. Johnnie chokes harder, harder even, and I feel my head turn hot. I drop the board and the wheels go wild.

Finally, he chucks me into a chair. I lean over the tub and toss; beer flushes out my nose.

"Talk," he orders.

I wipe my arm across my face. "Fuck you."

His fist nicks my jaw and I fall against the table. Leftover ung choy and mushrooms splatter to the floor. The bowl spins and spins until it stops. Johnnie throws a towel at my head. "Clean it up."

"No."

He puts out his butt on an empty soda can. "Clean it up."

I crouch and sweep the mess into the garbage. The vegetables fall apart like tofu in my fingers.

He knocks the heel of his shoe against the floor. "Just had to cause trouble, didn't you?"

Fuck off, I want to say. "You're just pissed."

"What was that?"

"P-i-s-s-e-d," I say. "Rich girl doesn't want Chinatown homeboy in her pants, does she?"

I block a punch. The blow stings. I look him in the eye, like, Go ahead, Asshole. I'll take you on.

There's a knock at the door. Johnnie pushes me aside and I trip over the board.

The first person I see is Billy. Then the cops. Two of them sandwiching him on either side. One of them's got his hand on Billy's shoulder, like he's all big

THE FIRST PERSON I SEE IS BILLY. THEN THE COPS.

and fatherlike.

"Is this the home of Eric Tsui?"

The precinct stinks of fat cops and old papers. It's puke-green and white. The plastic tiles are chipped at the corners and coming up in places; the windows are covered with a hundred years of dirt. Two squashed beer cans sit on the cop's desk. Evidence: one taken from my jacket pocket, the other labeled "weapon," which they probably found beneath some parked car. The things are separated into bags.

Johnnie says, "You really fucked up this time."

"Where's Ma?"

"She's not coming."

"You're an asshole, you know that?"

Johnnie comes at me, then, but all he gets is a weak jab at the shoulder before a cop pulls him away.

"Ungrateful little shit," Johnnie says. "She's at the hospital begging the old bastard not to press charges." He takes off, rushing down the stairs. "I hope they lock up your sorry ass and throw away the key," he says, slamming the door and leaving me alone at the precinct.

The cop pushes me into a chair. "Take it easy. A few questions, okay?"

My leg starts to tremble. If Ma was here, she'd say, "Stop shake. Shake luck away."

Half an hour goes by before Ma shows. She comes up to me, and just as I think I'm getting a hug, she stops, stares, then smacks me across the face. Her eyes puff. She signs whatever papers the cops give her, and we leave. Outside, Ma walks a step ahead. She sighs and shakes her head. I know what she's thinking. Things would be different if Dad was still around. If he hadn't up and died on us, we'd be okay right now.

"I'm sorry, Ma," I finally say. She sighs and shakes her head again.

At home, Ma shuts herself in her room. Johnnie's already in bed, so he doesn't fuck with me. He gives me a look like, Just you wait. I climb up to my bunk and pass out in my clothes.

It's still dark out when Ma shakes me awake. "Get up," she says.

There's the smell of fried eggs, which makes me want to toss. It isn't until I sit up that it all comes back. I climb off the bunk. Johnnie's still sleeping, his jaw open so that the world can see his gross white tongue. Ma's got a tray of food out. A mug of tea, an egg sandwich made with Wonder Bread, rice congee with a quartered thousand-year-old egg, wood chopsticks she gets from the restaurant, and a folded napkin.

"What's that?" I ask.

She makes an impatient throat-clearing sound and points downstairs. "Bring to Lao Gong," she whispers.

"No way I'm going into that rat hole."

She sniffles and watches me through puffy eyes.

"Smells like piss," I say. "You can smell it in the hallway."

"An old man," she mutters, sighing again. "All my fault. Didn't raise you good.

No, not a good mama."

"Ma, stop—that's not true."

"If only it had been me and not your father. He would have taught you right. He would have known what to do." The skin around her eyes looks like crumpled paper. She balances the tray with one hand. A blue vein swells at the inside of her elbow. "An old man. No one to help him. No one to buy food for him."

"The grocery drops stuff off every Friday."

"So smart. Know everything, hah? The grocery has new owner. No more deliveries anymore. The old man didn't eat for two days." She shakes her head and moves toward the door, balancing the tray on one arm like she does at work.

"Wait," I say, and then she hands the tray to me, adding a pad and pen.

"Make a list of things to buy. What he wants to eat later."

"You're going to shop for him now, too?" Ma's stare makes me nervous.

"You are."

Ma stands at the top of the stairs. "Careful—don't trip," she says.

"If I knew this would be the deal, I would've stayed in jail," I grumble. The tray jiggles unsteadily. Tea spills, soaking up the napkin.

"Not too late," she says.

The moldy old-people stink reaches me halfway down the stairs. My empty stomach flips upside down.

"Not too late," I mimic.

"Eh? What you say?" She crosses her arms over her chest.

"Nothing."

Outside Lao Gong's door, I listen for some kind of sound. The guy could be sleeping; he could be sitting in an easy chair with the cane resting across his lap, waiting for the littlest bit of noise. Who knows? He could have his ear up against the other side of the door.

"What you waiting for?" Ma snaps from above.

The tray wobbles, food slipping sideways. "Ma, will you go inside already?"

In front of me, the door swings open, and the first thing I see is the gauze bandage wrapped around the old man's head. A raw patch of scraped skin, swollen and black and blue, stands out on his cheek. He's still got that coat. There's a tear at the pocket.

"Hello," I say.

"Hello, Lao Gong," Ma corrects. Gritting my teeth, I force myself to repeat after her.

The old man stares at me blankly. He blinks slowly and scratches his head like he doesn't have a clue why the hell I'm here.

"E-lic?" he finally says.

"Yep."

"Ah?"

"Eric."

"E-lic," he says, leaning against the door jamb, then switching into Cantonese: "You're standing on my newspaper." I step back. His hand shakes as he bends down for the thing. Without another word, he places it on a stack by the door, then disappears into the darkness.

One step and I bang into a wall of newspapers and nearly drop the tray. It takes a second for my eyes to adjust, and when they do, I can make out the piles that line the hallway on both sides. There's a sticky warm feeling, the kind you get when you never open a window. "Lao Gong?"

I find him in the main room. The layout's the same as ours: tub dead center in the kitchen. In the corner, a large cot stacked with more newspapers. There's only one clear path, which goes from hallway to desk and desk to bathtub. The rod above the tub has metal links but no curtain. A towel and one set of underwear—old and see-through—hang from the rim of the tub.

The old man's at his desk, poring over a paper with a magnifying glass. There's a small lamp, the kind with a pull-on, pull-off tassel, and a black-and-white picture of a woman with small, fuzzy eyes. He turns the page, and under the light, I see dust rising into the air. The newspapers are yellowed and frayed. "So much work," he says. "Must hurry, hurry."

I check out the stacks that cover the floor. "Guess you like newspapers, huh?"

He looks at the room as if it's the first time he's really seeing what's in front of him, then turns to the woman in the picture. "Sitting here all these years," he says. "No time to look at them."

What the hell's he been so busy doing all day? I wonder.

"So much to do, now," he says. A headline in the paper catches his attention. "Ah yah, those no-good Communists."

I place the tray on the table. Half the tea has spilled. "Careful," he says. "Don't mess the newspaper." His teeth are so big and white, so perfect compared to the rest of his face. There's no way they can be real.

"Ah? What do we have here?" he asks.

"Breakfast."

"What's that? Speak up." He notices me staring at the bandage and fidgets with it the way you do your nose when someone stares at it too long. For a minute, I almost like the guy. He mixes the thousand-year-old egg into the congee, stirs it with the chopsticks and slurps from the bowl. Black egg dribbles from the corner of his mouth, and I can't watch anymore. The newspaper's turned to an article headlined HO CHI MINH MAKES DEAL WITH MAO. The thing's dated October 3, 1958. Way, way older than me.

When he's finished eating, Lao Gong makes a sucking noise through his teeth. "Not bad," he says, setting the empty bowl back on the tray and drawing the mug of tea to his mouth. He takes a sip, and when he places the mug back on the table, congee shit is floating on the surface.

"Ma said you needed food?"

Lao Gong examines the next page. The heading reads NATIONALISTS FLEE TACHEN ISLANDS. "Ai," he mutters. "Those Communists. We have to fight. Fight, I say. Don't you agree?"

"Guess so."

He drops the magnifying glass to the table. "Guess so? Guess so?" Spit hits me in the eye and I back off. Whacked, I think.

His eyes go blank again. "Chow fun," he says, licking his lips. "Across the street. Old man Ho cheaper." He reaches beneath layers of clothes and pulls out a small change purse that Ma might use. Lao Gong hands me two dollars and seven cents.

"Beef?" I ask.

"Shrimp. Lots of chili sauce. And soy milk. Yes, ah. Soy milk." He digs into his clothes again and pulls out the door key.

I take off and get back with the carton of noodles in less than ten minutes. When I walk in, I hear the guy yammering away to himself. "Soon, any day. We'll run those Communist scoundrels away and then we'll go home for a look-see." By the time I make it to the main room, the old man is quiet again, the magnifying glass moving from top to bottom of the page, and from right to left.

Ma gets a kick out of the whole thing. "So?" she asks.

I circle a finger at my temple. "Cuckoo… Cuckoo. Goes on and on about Communism. How we gotta fight."

"Poor man. At the hospital, he was all confused. Thought I was his dead wife." She unravels the apron and checks to see if it needs a wash. She tries to press out a wrinkle.

"I'm telling you," I say. "The old man's loopy in the head. It's like a garbage dump down there."

"Comes from a village down south," Ma says. "Likely that they ran away before the Communists—kept talking about taking her home one day." She sighs and settles into the chair, turning on the TV. The only thing that's on is the news.

Johnnie comes out of the toilet. He's dressed in one of those preppy plaid shirts with too much pink. "Damn troublemaker," he says. "Ma should have let you rot."

"Johnnie," she warns.

"Like I give a shit what you think?" I say.

Ma jumps between us. She does one of

where Quemoy is or even who those Communists really are. Through the magnifying glass, the characters get as large as nickels. Ma took Lao Gong to the doctor's yesterday, and though he's still got the bandage, it isn't as large or thick as the last one. Soft baby hair pokes out from beneath the gauze.

For the first time, I notice the thump of footsteps upstairs. Johnnie's plastic

THE BIGGER PART OF ME FEELS SORRY TO BE ALIVE; SORRY TO BE ONE OF THE DISAPPOINTMENTS IN HER LIFE.

her so-tired-so-tired sighs.

"You two. It's New Year's. Bad luck to fight."

A part of me wants to shake the hell out of her. The bigger part of me feels sorry to be alive; sorry to be one of the disappointments in her life. I grab my knapsack and board, and before Ma has the chance to say anything else, I'm out of there.

Weeks later, when I get back from the bakery with a tsoa su bao, the old man's going on about the Islands of Quemoy. "Those Communists," he says. "Can you believe this? Rascals, I tell you."

I nod, even though I don't have any idea

slippers. He's headed down the hallway to the toilet. I borrow the cane propped at the side of the desk and move slowly toward the bathroom. When I hear the first squeak of a fart, I bang the cane against the ceiling.

Johnnie curses. I hear him jump off the toilet. "What the heck?"

I don't want him to hear me laughing, so I make my way back to the main room. Lao Gong turns the page. Hasn't heard a thing, I think, slipping the cane back on the desk. He looks up, then;

looks through the glass at me. His eye is huge like the Cyclops dude we read about in school.

"That wasn't right," he says, folding the paper and placing it on the finished-reading pile. "For maximum effect, hold end like this. Bang with handle."

I'm like, What'd he say? But Lao Gong goes back to reading the next paper, and when he does so, it's like I'm not there anymore.

The bruise Johnnie gave me covers four ribs on my left side. I don't give the Asshole the time of day. Act like it was nothing, didn't hurt, don't even remember getting the thing. The old man's reading the latest about Nixon. "What a good man," he says. "Such a good president." The bandage came off yesterday, and because of the uneven patches of hair, Ma razed his head, the whole thing. It's like the shell of a salted duck egg.

I hand him the tray of tea and sa ping yiu tiao. Lao Gong bites into the fried dough, chews quickly, swallows. Grease sneaks down the side of his mouth.

"What do you want me to get for lunch?" I ask.

"Buy? Oh, yes. Let me think."

I tap my foot. "Min fen?"

"Not today."

"Chow fun?"

He makes that whistly sound through his teeth. "Didn't I have that yesterday?"

"No. Gai lan and fish."

"Ah? I did? No, can't be."

"How about spare ribs?"

"Spare ribs, spare ribs." He stops to consider it a moment, but his gaze fixes on the article again. He shakes his head. "Ai, yah. This Watergate. What's so big deal? Simple. Just chop fingers, then no more burgle." He flips through the paper.

Crazy old man. I give in and sit on the finished-reading pile. Lao Gong calls it the throwaway pile, and now it's me who gets to do the dumping. The room is the same, nothing more, nothing less, except every day there are fewer newspapers. The path to the tub is wider; the read stacks by the desk taller.

"How come you waited so long to read these?" I ask.

"Very busy," he says. "You don't know. After my wife died . . ."

The sound of the word stuns him.

"Lao Gong?"

"Thinking," he says, smoothing a hand over the newspaper. "Thinking, thinking."

Shit, I think, cause I know what he means. When Dad died, nothing else mattered. Dust rises from the desk. The specks drift under the lamplight.

"Don't you ever get lonely in this place?" I ask.

"Lonely?"

"I mean, don't you got friends or anything? Family?"

He blinks, then sweeps his arm over the room of papers. "*This* is my family."

"Newspapers?"

"Ah."

I shake my head. "I don't get it. I mean, where do you sleep?"

"You see, you see?" he says, ignoring my question and pointing to another article. "Those Americans not so stupid after all. Hospitals using acupuncture to anesthetize patients before surgery. See? They're learning. Eastern medicine much better." He rubs the back of his head where he got the stitches.

"Lao Gong?"

"Ah?"

"Where do you sleep?"

He looks about the room, then up at me. "Why, here, the desk, of course."

"On top? Just like that?"

"What kind of question is that? Floor so dusty. Not possible."

"But why don't you sleep in bed?"

He places the magnifying glass onto the paper. "Then no place for newspapers. This here is enough. Bed so big. Too big

for one person." He shakes his head at the woman in the photo. "Young people. Can't tell when they see a busy man. No worry. Soon, I come, ah?" He touches the picture frame.

Come where? I wonder. What a spook.

After school, Billy's like, What do you mean you got things to do? He wants to head to Astor where a bunch of thrashers hang out. I don't tell him the Asshole came after me this morning cause I took my sweet time taking a dump. Said I was going to make him late for a job interview, but I knew it was 'cause of the girl. He called last night and couldn't get past her father.

My side throbs. "Got things to do," I say.

"Come on—it's not like I shouldn't be getting to the store. We'll hang for an hour. What's an hour?"

A green Volvo passes us, nearly swiping Billy's leg. He punches the trunk. "Fucking idiot Jersey drivers," he says. "So? Coming or what?"

"The old man," I say. "Gotta take him to the doctor's. Ma's got day-shift today."

"Fuck him."

"Shut up, man."

"You getting soft on me?"

"I said, shut up." A pain stabs me between the ribs and I wince.

Billy backs off. I don't have to say anything else. He knows, and he's thinking, We should have pegged the Asshole when we had the chance. I try to smile.

"Well, catch you later," he finally says. "Watch your back, man."

"Yep, later." I drop the board to the ground, and even though each bump feels like a knife sticking me in the ribs, I skate all the way home.

I can hear the guy rambling as soon as I walk in the door. "Can you believe? The *president*. Ai, no respect, these Americans."

"Hello?" I whisper.

"Ah? What you say? Speak louder, Si-mong."

"Lao Gong?" I say, my sneakers thudding against the floor. "Ready to go?"

He places the photo back on the desk and looks at me. "Go, ah?"

"The doctor."

He nods, ignoring what I've said, then taps at Nixon's face in the paper. "Ah, E-lic. Sit here. Look how Americans want to impeach their own president. So shame. Don't you think?"

"Guess so."

"Guess so? Guess so?"

Shit, not again. "Yes, I mean, yes."

"Ah. Shameless, these reporters. So

what he lies, ah? Good man, that Nixon. Smart. No one else goes to China. Now, look. Open doors, ah?" He stares at me through the magnifying glass and blinks. "We have to do something," he says, a hand over his chest. "Chinese for Nixon, ah?"

It's going to take a million years for this guy to catch up, I think. He goes back to finish the article, whispers to himself as if he were praying.

The room looks different. Newspapers remain piled on the bed and arc around the bathtub, but the pathways seem wider. The throwaway piles by the desk get higher and higher. Lao Gong says, "Hurry. No time, ah? Have to finish." Every day, now, I take the papers he's read to the basement, dump them in the fryer, and watch the stuff burn.

Today, when I try to lift the papers, a sharp pain twitches at my side, and I drop the stuff. I can't even breathe. Quickly, before he notices, I gather the newspaper back into a neat pile.

Lao Gong places the magnifying glass on the desk. "E-lic, ah?"

"What?"

"Doctor," he says, using the cane to push himself up.

"Doctor?" My face gets hot. Who, *me*?

He shakes his head. "Ai, didn't you say

I'm going to be late?"

Air fills me up again. "Yep," I say. "That's right."

Johnnie starts up first thing in the morning. I know it's coming because he didn't get the job. I'm on the can, thinking about some whack dream I had. There are only bits and pieces, like, I'm in a bathtub, sleeping. The thing's filled with water. My side beats like a heart. It opens up and a rib, cooked with spicy barbecue sauce, comes out. But then what happened?

In the kitchen, Ma's stir-frying beef in oyster sauce for us to warm later. The smoky smell reaches me at the end of the hall. The popping sound, the burning oil, was in the dream, too, somehow.

Slippers flap against the floor. Johnnie pounds against the door. "Hey," he says. "Get the hell out, already."

"I'm taking a shit. Too bad." I love it in here, I think. A closet with a sturdy lock.

He kicks the door.

I hear Ma say, "Ai. You two. Why always fight? Fight, fight. Mama so tire." Johnnie shuts his face. I wipe and pull on my jeans, but by the time I get out, it's too late. The front door shuts and Ma's gone.

"See what you did?" Johnnie says.

"Shut up."

He grabs me by the cuff of my shirt.

"Say it again. Go ahead. Say it."

I look him in the face and what I see is the loser who always wants the girl he can't get or the job no Chinatown home-boy's going to ollie up, and when he stares back at me, his nose all swollen and pink with hate, I know he sees the part of him he hates most, the part he won't ever be able to get rid of. And somehow, I know the old man's standing in his hallway, right below our feet. He's listening. Waiting. His cane is handle side up in the air, ready to knock against the ceiling.

Before the Asshole lands his first swing, I say, "You fucking lose, man. You really do."

By the time I make it down to Lao Gong's place, it's already too late to meet up with Billy before school, anyway. I've got the board in one hand, the tray of tea and congee, beef and yellow radish in the other. A hamburger the size of a Big Mac covers my right eye. It's hard to blink, the thing waters so much, but it doesn't hurt. Nothing does.

If Lao Gong brings it up—if he says, I was knocking and knocking but noise didn't stop—I'll say, I don't know what you're talking about; I'll say, mind your own damn business, old man. This got nothing to do with you. The only ba-lalang going on around here, I'll say, is in your big, fat head.

The food Ma made smells sort of sweet. It goes up my nose and makes me sick.

Before I get to the bottom of the stairs, I notice the newspaper still on the mat outside the old man's door. Shit, I think. He up and died. Just like that. Up and died on me, the fucker.

I leave my board at the front door and let myself in. That's when I really freak. The piles of newspaper over the floor and bed are gone. What's left is in the toss piles around the desk and chair. The lamp is still on. A magnifying glass sits on the tabletop.

"Lao Gong?"

The bumpy linoleum is covered with clouds of dust. The tub sits empty in the middle of the room. Underwear hangs from the rack. Lao Gong lies on the bed in the corner of the room. He holds the picture close to his face. I place the tray on the floor and step closer to the bed.

"Lao Gong?" I whisper. "Hello?"

"Ah?" He doesn't open his eyes. "Yes, soon," he says.

"What's soon?"

"So much to do."

I look at the empty room. One large tub, a bed, the desk. The floor is more uneven than ours. By the leg of the bed, a tile is missing. "It's finished," I say.

He smiles and hugs tighter to the picture frame. "Soon, I come home, ah? Yes, yes. Come, now. We go home."

I start with the piles around the desk, moving them to the basement. Downstairs, there's a moistness that smells moldy, like new rot. I open the furnace and feed each bundle to the fire. The flame singes the edges, first, then catches like burning souls. My hands get covered with ink; my skin stinks of fire.

It takes three hours to toss all the papers. When they're all gone, I go back upstairs and watch the guy sleeping. His hair has grown back silver and straight. Three months, and all of a sudden, he seems too small in that gray coat.

The desk is clear except for the lamp, magnifying glass, and cane. I place the tray of food on the table. The tea is cold. I brush my hand over the desk. What would it be like to sleep here? Here, alone, on this hard, smooth desk. I hug the board to my chest, spin a wheel, and decide on a bowl of Shanghai noodles and soup dumplings.

I shut the door and let the old man sleep. 🏠

CONFESSIONS OF AN UNREPENTANT EXILE

. . . .

ALBERTO FUGUET ON ARIEL DORFMAN

During the week of Chilean dictator Pinochet's arrest in London, an emerging young Santiago-based novelist and Tin House Contributing Editor talks about Chile's cultural schizophrenia with the country's number one exile, novelist, playwright and longtime thorn in the side of his country's military dictatorship.

Ariel Dorfman is an interviewer's dream. You turn on a tape recorder and he flies on *piloto automatico*. Every phrase he utters is a sound bite. Just say "your book" and he dazzles you. Say "Chile" or "Pinochet" and you can spend the rest of the day knowing your blank tape will soak up Op-Ed copy.

I, like Dorfman, come from Chile. You can't go farther south than that. I'm not talking Interstate-accessible, pickled-egg, deep fried South. I'm talking next-stop-South-Pole South. But Dorfman is not in Chile, though he goes there frequently. He lives in Durham, North Carolina. So I went to the *northern* South to see my *compatriota*. I wanted to see if, in the States, he seemed as fish-out-of-water as he does in Chile, where he looms over everyone like a whale in pond. I wondered how he would sound, react, and swim in a world where everything is in English and the stench of authoritarianism does not fill the air.

Perhaps I should introduce myself. Hi, nice to meet you, as they say here. English used to be my playground. I was made in the U.S.A. by Chilean parents, though I ended up being born in Santiago. I was back in the States when I was only a couple of months old. I grew up in Encino, California. No place for a writer, true. It didn't really matter since it hardly occurred to me to be one. Why? I mean, I lived in the Valley. That's why. We had the Galleria, the beach, the cul-de-sacs, Ventura Boulevard. The Bradys and the Partridges lived in a house like ours. Vonda Shephard went to my elementary school. Disneyland was close, so was Burbank. Life was good, with no subtitles.

When Salvador Allende was overthrown in 1973 by a CIA-backed coup, Ariel Dorfman fled Chile and, amazingly, my family and I went back. Not immediately. It started out as a summer vacation. A Fourth of July. I saw fireworks as we flew over the Panama Canal. I never returned to the United States—at least not as a permanent resident.

At night, Durham resembles Santiago during the *protestas*, when blackouts and curfew invaded the night. Empty, silent, pitch-dark. You don't see a thing. It's safe, though, except for the squirrels. And the deer.

I arrived at Dorfman's little literary/anti-Pinochet war room in the middle of the woods at Duke University, where he teaches one semester a year. Pinochet had just been imprisoned in London, and Dorfman had been churning out columns and open letters aimed at furthering his agenda.

"Last week I had a very interesting experience," Dorfman says, as he goes over a fax that must get through to England. "An experience of crisis. When I'm in crisis, the country is in crisis, the human-rights community is in crisis—this due to the Pinochet thing. I had to write an article for *El Pais*, which is the most important paper of the Spanish-speaking world. I thought: That's fine, I'll write it for them in Spanish, of course, then I'll write the same thing in English for the *L.A. Times* or for some paper in England. What I discovered was that it was not translatable. What I had to write–an open letter to Pinochet—I just couldn't write in English. And when I wrote a piece for the *Evening Standard*, I

At night, Durham resembles Santiago during the protestas, when blackouts and curfew invaded the night.

realized that I had to separate the English from the Spanish and I had to speak to an audience of English speakers in a different way than to an audience of Spanish speakers. This crisis, then, reopens borders that I thought were shut."

Not only for Dorfman, but for me and all Chileans, Pinochet's imprisonment has split open a wound that many thought—or had hoped–was stitched and closed.

"Chile is a country that is full of false certitudes and sham reconciliations," says Dorfman. He explains how his new book, a fascinating literary and political memoir, *Heading South, Looking North: A Bilingual Journey*, confronts this unfortunate reality: "My memoir says, You know what? You guys are lying to each other. What I do in this book is, along with understanding some of the failures that we had, I glorify them. I celebrate them. I think those were the best days of my life and I say so. I also say, These are the mistakes that I made. Not that *we* made but

> "Chile is a country that is full of false certitudes and sham reconciliations."

that *I* made. Personally. It's very easy to say, Well, we were *sectarios*, sectarian: we cared more about ourselves than about others. Hold it, I say. With whom were you *sectario*? Give me the name, the address. Who did you hurt, concretely? Okay, now let's talk. I think that is what the country needs to do."

Ariel Dorfman's relationship with Chile is a complex one. He's more devoted to the country than the country to him. He definitely loves the place and, as all writers should, loathes it with his guts.

Dorfman was actually born in Argentina to Russian Jewish Communist parents and raised in the shadow of the United Nations in Manhattan. His family settled in Chile when Dorfman was twelve years old. Twenty years later, working as a cultural advisor to Allende's government, Dorfman found himself a hair away from death when Pinochet rocketed his way into power. His diasporic early life has led Dorfman to label himself as "a hybrid, part Yankee, part Chilean, a pinch of Jew, a mestizo in search of a center," a search he describes at length in *Heading South, Looking North*.

Though still a Chilean citizen, Dorfman left Chile twenty-five years ago and, for many of those years, was not allowed back in. "They had been describing me this way," he says. "'Ariel Dorfman was exiled from Chile after the coup against Salvador Allende.' That was the way they presented me. And I said, 'No, I'm not an exile anymore. I just don't want to go back.' For an exile, politics is more

Alberto Fuguet and Ariel Dorfman in Durham, October 1998

important than literature. For an expatriate, it's the contrary."

Chile, like many countries, is divided into three slices–the Right, the center and the Left–each with 33 percent of the vote, putting the center at the center of every storm. The Left's intelligentsia, the ones who are internationally connected and are part of the coalition democratic government, are the Red Set. Our own Radical Chic. One would think they're Dorfman's people. They are not. In general, his literary peers in Chile disavow him, do not consider him one of them. In fact, he is overlooked by Chile's establishment, both Right and Left. Perhaps it's envy, perhaps it's the stale but still lingering anti-American sentiment, but it's there.

Maybe it's his bravado. Dorfman has been quoted in interviews saying things like this: "My poems, for example, are not available in Chile. There have been twenty anthologies of Chilean poetry and I'm not in any of them. I'm in *The Hundred Most Significant Poems of the Twentieth Century*. My poems are read by Meryl Streep, by Peggy Ashcroft; Julia Roberts wants to read them for a record we might be doing. But they are not available in Chile. Look, at this moment we are producing a half-hour fictional special for British television—with some of the great actors of the world and a wonderful director—which is going to be transmitted in perhaps seventy countries. They are selling the rights like hot cakes."

People in Chile don't talk like that. Literary people are embarrassed to talk about the advance they did not get. One just does not behave that way. A writer who doesn't let me use his name (many are afraid of Dorfman and his connections—all go off the record, as if he was with the CIA) tells me that, overall, it's the name-dropping that does him in. And for Chileans, it is worse because the names are often unfamiliar, making people feel out of the loop.

When the Red Set brainstormed the political opposition's TV campaign, the one that, in 1989, overthrew by votes Pinochet's guns, Dorfman convinced several American stars to campaign for the cause: Christopher Reeve, I recall, Richard Dreyfuss, Glenn Close. "That was just plain show-off," said an under-sold Chilean writer friend of mine. "Yes, it's envy, but it's a healthy envy. *Envidia sana*. A Chilean envy. Dorfman knows how we are and, yet, he does it anyway. He should know better. He dares us and ends up losing."

Dorfman's latest dare was to take big names to Chile and organize a literary conference that celebrated the Southern Hemisphere. All this in the middle of the English Patient storm (that's what the tabloids call the Pinochet-sick-and-under-arrest-in-London episode). Nadine Gordimer, Peter Carey, André Brink, among others, flew down. Few Chileans showed up and no important local writers assisted.

As my undersold Chilean writer friend puts it, "Dorfman is box-office poison in Chile. His torture play lasted a week. The Polanski movie, based on the play, bombed. He's a one-note lobbyist and I envy his contacts. Imagine what I could do with them."

Dorfman's reviews in the Chilean media are predictable. His memoir was slammed with crude, nasty reviews that were down-right personal. One of them said: "He's famous so he knows that whatever he writes will get published, no matter how badly written." In the States they say quite the opposite.

"I think with few exceptions, nobody has really *read* me in Chile," Dorfman says. "Nobody has the slightest idea of who I really am. They have both a legendary and diabolical vision of an Ariel Dorfman who has fame outside of Chile, which he doesn't deserve. I'm probably the best-known unread author in Chile." He takes a deep breath and continues. "Because I was so political, I was always put into a category of 'His things are contingent and therefore their worth depends on his political work.' The image I gave out was that of a person whose success was due to his politics and not to his writing, when I think that my success is due to the opposite: in spite of my politics, in this country I've managed to carve a place for myself. I'm not saying that the Left does not have a certain strength, but there are things that I say in my memoir that are not gratifying for North Americans, either.

"So," he continues, "I think that the bringing together of politics and literature, in the aesthetic way that I do it, where I think that *both* have a space, that is what is unforgivable: that I'm trying to do something extremely ambitious and very different. When the Chilean transition came, I wrote *Death and the Maiden* rather than doing what many of the writers were doing, which was forgetting the past. And my own wife, who rarely makes a mistake, said: 'You really want to write about a torture victim?' And I said: 'It's really about silence, it's about lying, it's about deception, about the fractures of the country.'

"It's about memory," Dorfman adds. "It deals with torture because that was what happened to certain people. I think I have to tell that story because nobody else is telling it. Talent entails responsibility. I have the power of the word, I don't want

"I think I have to tell that story because nobody else is telling it. Talent entails responsibility. I have the power of the word, I don't want to misuse that. I'm obsessed with that. Words are not only the ones you write, but the ones you engage."

to misuse that. I'm obsessed with that. Words are not only the ones you write, but the ones you engage. Since I was a child, I've absorbed pain as a sponge. It just comes into me and I can't get rid of it. When that happens, I get indignant. I try to make the world a better place. So if Pinochet is under custody, I feel I must speak out."

Some say that Dorfman means no harm, that he just turned into a gringo and, as such, lost his touch with Chile's local customs and its current zeitgeist. An example, perhaps, is the Amnesty International rock concert I attended in Mendoza, Argentina in 1989. It was Amnesty's Chile concert on the Human Rights Now tour but it took place on the other side of the Andes because Pinochet didn't allow the rockers-with-a-message inside Chile. Dorfman appeared on stage just before Sting, his "amigo," and began reading a poem that dealt with death and torture. Most of the kids in the stadium booed. They wanted to rock. Sure, most of them were rebellious and anti-dictatorship, but a lot weren't. One of them was a right-wing pro-Pinochet friend of mine who hates Dorfman, though he has never read one of his books. He blames people like Dorfman for the fact that Pinochet is in jail.

This friend of mine wrote me an E-mail contending, "[Dorfman] and his American politically correct, bleeding-heart pals. If only *our* people could speak English so well, could have his clout, his prestige, Dorfman would be the one behind bars, not Pinochet. He is part of the socialist conspiracy. Instead of trying to erase Pinochet from the face of the earth, he should thank him. If it weren't for his beca, that exile-scholarship that kicked him out of Chile, he'd still be stuck in Santiago. Pinochet made him. He owes him his career. No Pinochet, no Dorfman."

Dorfman, I think, would enjoy this comment. He thrives on this sort of attack.

"I used to ask a friend of mine in Chile to send me all the reviews, especially the bad ones, because I was a masochist," Dorfman says. "Now I ask him to send

them to me because I'm a sadist. When you have sixty reviews of your work, from Jerusalem to Brazil, and some of the greatest writers in the world saying that this is an extraordinary work, I almost enjoy the fact of some small soul in *El Mercurio* saying that this is worthless, basically. That it's badly written, that it's not lyrical."

"You think it's a Chilean thing?" I ask.

"You know," he replies, "I think some people *are* prophets in their own land. I think Chile has a particular problem with the outside world. We invented the word *chaqueteo*. *Chaqueteo* means to grab someone's jacket. Why do you grab someone from the jacket? It's because they have gone up a bit further than they should. So you grab the guy from the jacket and pull him down, where he belongs. I'd be very happy if I was more appreciated in Chile, but what can I do?"

Dorfman and I talked a lot in Durham, he more than I. We talked in English, which was a little odd and, for me at least, sort of *arriviste*, but his new book was, after all, in English and we were in the

> *"I used to ask a friend of mine in Chile to send me all the reviews, especially the bad ones, because I was a masochist," Dorfman says. "Now I ask him to send them to me because I'm a sadist."*

States. In Chile, I would have never dared to speak in *Inglés. Ni cagando.*

"Our relationship has always been in Spanish, true," Dorfman says as he discreetly places a cushion behind his back. "But behind our Spanish-language relationship, when we talk in *Chileno*, I think that we were always aware, from the very start, of the English infiltration into our Spanish. So though we were speaking in Spanish to each other, we were aware that each of us had a U.S. dimension to our life. A lot of the conversations we've had have been about the difficulty of living in two societies, two cultures. . . . My advice to you has always been that you should write in English."

True–though, after reading Dorfman's *Heading South, Looking North*, in which he insightfully delves into his linguistic masala, I've come to the following conclusion: Dorfman is bilingual and I am not. You win some, you lose some. Perhaps I suffered the madness of being double but in my case, Spanish won.

I ask Dorfman if he considers himself truly bilingual.

"Yes, I am," he replies. "I understand the truly bilingual person as the one who has two mother tongues. Not having a mother tongue and a stepmother tongue, which might be your case. You are in love with one language and you flirt with the other one. One is your wife and the other is your lover."

So I'm flirting. And, coming not only from a Catholic country but from the only country in the world with no divorce law, I understand how painful, empowering, slippery, and fun adultery can be. I tell Dorfman that. I tell him that in English he seems freer, almost playful.

"Yes, because the solemnity of my life has been lived in Spanish. My dead are Spanish-speaking dead," he says. "I don't have any English-speaking dead. . . . What I discovered was this: it was about containing the emotion of what I had lived. And it came simultaneously with my discovery of my story's structure, because the structure has as its spine my encounters with death in Chile, which I lived in Spanish. So to write that in Spanish I think would have been a mistake. Some of the critiques that I do of myself, of my positions in the past and of Chile in general, are so strong that when I began to translate this into Spanish, I literally began to tremble saying: I cannot have written this."

"So it's true that in Spanish you're more, say, solemn?" I ask.

"I have never been able to write a comedy in Spanish, never," Dorfman replies. "There can be some funny things in them but they are tragic books. *Who's Who*, my new play, I wrote directly in English. It's a tragic farce about Hollywood. A dark comedy. I began to write it in Spanish by myself. It was about Chile and it didn't work out. It was called *Paginas Sociales*. It was about an old woman who was in charge of the social pages of a paper like *El Mercurio* who thinks everybody wants to kill her. And I couldn't. It didn't work in Spanish. I was desperate. Then one night my wife said to me, 'You know what's the matter? This shouldn't be about Chile. It should be about Hollywood. It should be about a casting director.' I then realized I could only do this with my son. And we did it in English. I can only write comedy in English. My newest novel, *The Nanny and the Iceberg*, is in English and it's outrageously funny."

"Is it about Chile?"

"Yes. In fact it's the first realistic book I've written about Chile. I've always been allegorical in Spanish about Chile. But this is the first time I've written about real people. I have dates, streets, concrete things about Chile. But I wrote it in English. That novel is narrated by a young Chilean who, at six years old, left the country for the States, and returned to Chile when he is twenty-three. Sound familiar?" asks Dorfman.

Yes it does, though I was not, like Dorf-man's character, twenty-three when I moved to Chile. I was, like Dorfman himself, twelve. A bad age to go Third World, welcome to the dictatorship, gringo go home. I wished. To go home. But I stayed down there. Learned one language, lost another. Sort of. Turned into a writer. *En un escritor.* You have to learn the language somehow. When I come to the U.S., I feel comfortable but foreign. I like it more on TV and in the magazines I subscribe to. I'm ashamed that my surfer-dude accent turned into a Taco Bell one. *Hay cosas peores, supongo.* I do have a good Chilean accent. Dorfman, on the other hand, nails both accents with a vengeance, which is only one of the reasons I tip my hat to him.

My father also likes Dorfman, but then he likes Pinochet, too. My father lives in Orange County, California. "O.C.", as he calls it. He's an American citizen now. He followed my mother down to Chile and, after a couple of years, left us and headed back to the U.S. Long story. Bilingual, transcontinental breakup. My father is a blue-collar guy, delivers bread–Wonder Bread, doughnuts, bagels. Wears a uniform with a name tag on it. He is not a reader. I'm pretty sure he has barely read my stuff. When he does read, it's news and it's in English. When my father lived in Chile, Pinochet was king and my father enjoyed him. He thought he was funny, had charisma, *mano dura*. But my father skipped so many years of Chilean life that, to be fair, he probably didn't understand Pinochet.

As I said, my father also admires Ariel Dorfman. (It was my father's idea to go the mall and see *Death and the Maiden*. He laughed when Sigourney Weaver used Chilean matches—the ones with a picture of the Andes on the cover.) My father is proud of Dorfman. He feels Dorfman represents him. What little my father knows about current events in Chile, he knows from Dorfman. *Es re-capo ese Dorfman.* Dorfman has appeared on *Nightline* with Ted Koppel, on CNN, in the newspapers. My father admires his English. His ease. My father once said to me: "Are you going to be like Dorfman—be on TV, in English?" So when Dorfman makes his Zelig-like appearances, my dad turns to him.

My father called me years ago to ask me about Rodrigo Rojas. He was upset: He'd heard—in the States via Dorfman—about Rojas, a mixed-up Chilean teenager raised in the D.C. suburbs who, during the eighties, went to Santiago to find himself but instead found a terrible end. "What was going on around there?" my father wanted to know. "Don't get mixed up in politics: those guys are ruthless." My dad knew more about Rojas than he knew about me;

he knew Rojas was a photographer—at least wanted to be one; he knew that on one of the protest days, those days when Pinochet's soldiers took to the streets and students like me either threw rocks or scrambled, Rojas, armed with his bad Spanish and a too-shiny, too-visible camera, followed the flow, snapping away, and, in an alley, was burned to death by young soldiers barely drafted.

Dorfman had used all his power in the U.S. to expose Rojas's murder. And he got to my dad. It was also one of the few occasions that my dad got to me.

Dorfman writes in *Heading South, Looking North*: "My Latin American masters had elbowed their way into those prestigious foreign peaks that I aspired to, that my writing sought to reach, and they had done so using the Spanish I still refused to consider the language of my literary destiny. But, instead of taking that success as proof that if I wanted to be universally recognized, Spanish was as advantageous an instrument as English, I construed the whole phenomenon quite differently. These were the facts: there existed, for the first time in the history of Latin America, a literature that could speak to its own readers, while simultaneously appealing to a vast public abroad, and this literary movement asserted that in order to be Latin

American you did not have to reject the international. I interpreted these facts as a green light for my bizarre experiment, the peculiar way in which I combined the native and the foreign, the national and the transcultural, the Spanish everyday experience and the English reelaboration at night. I thought that I could become the first Latin American writer to address the United States and Europe directly in English, without any need of translation."

Dorfman has, I believe, found a center and a linguistic home in the United States and with English. The same country and language, not coincidentally, of his childhood.

"The memoir has put me at peace with Chile," he tells me. "I have come to the conclusion that I want to be normally exasperated with the country, not *abnormally* exasperated."

I don't blame Dorfman for being exasperated. It's quite easy to get that way. Chile has an insular way of dealing with things. It seems Dorfman's persona non grata status will never be erased from his passport.

"I feel more at ease in South Africa than in Chile," says Dorfman. "I'm welcomed there the way I'm not welcomed in Chile. I think it has to do with the following: South Africa is a country that is in a

desperate search for its identity. It's a country that is trying to figure out what those years of dictatorship did to it. And, in Chile, we have turned our backs on trying to figure it out. So I see Pinochet's arrest as our chance to re-look at ourselves. It's shown the very ugly face of many people in the last few days. Death threats are beginning again. It's very interesting to see, all of a sudden, the civilized veneer of the country come off. We look at each other, without Pinochet present, and it's not a pretty sight. He has, in a sense, forced us into this juxtaposition, which is uneasy but quite healthy. We have to recognize the division and, until now, we hadn't."

I open my underlined copy of *Heading South, Looking North*. I ask Dorfman to sign it. I try to acquire as many signed books as I can.

He writes: *Para Alberto, este viaje que es tuyo y que, sin embargo, no es un modelo para nadie Con el canno bilingue de, Ariel.* "This journey is also yours, yet it should be no one's." Not a path to tread. Something like that. Dorfman's path was not a shiny one, nor has it been easy.

I ask him if he has any regrets.

"No," he says. "In fact, originally I was thinking of calling my memoir 'Confessions of an Unrepentant Exile'. So, no, there are no regrets."

ROMAN POLANSKI

ARIEL DORFMAN

The author of 'Death and the Maiden' observes the on-set obsessions that drive director Roman Polanski as he transforms the stage drama into film.

Something is wrong with the lamp. Roman examines it carefully. We are only a few days away from principal photography, but Roman Polanski acts as if he had all the time in the world. It is an ordinary kerosene lamp, the swinging sort you take on camping trips or you carry around the house when there's a blackout, the sort you would never give a second glance to. But Roman is giving it more than a second glance. He is spending long silent valuable minutes, observing it as if it were about to come alive and pounce on him.

We are on the set of *Death and the Maiden* in the studios of Boulogne, just outside Paris. The legendary art director Pierre Guffroy (a regular on many Polanski films, including *Tess*, for which he received an Academy Award) has painstakingly recreated a Latin American beach house down to the last detail. It is what Roman loves in Guffroy's work, enhanced and fine-tuned during a career at the service of Cocteau, Buñuel, and Bresson: the set is a character that whispers, shifts, lies in ambush, assists the protagonists, betrays them, comments on their blindness and hopes. And every object in that house—all the props that Roman is now inspecting with an unrelenting gaze—must blend into that atmosphere, must be consistent. Polanski puts the lamp down, then picks it up again, touches it, turns it around. It is almost as if he suspects the lamp of trickery, as if it were about to pull a fast one on him, like a fraudulent second-rate actor trying out for a starring role when he doesn't even deserve to be an extra. Roman looks up at the four or five people who surround him, who have been watching him watch the elusive lamp. He does not want help. He intends to figure this one out by himself. Briefly, his eyes fall on me. But they do not ask

anything, do not confirm or interrogate. Has he guessed that I happen to know what's wrong with the lamp? Not because I am especially good at visuals. In fact, overly devoted as I am to words and literature, I tend to be extremely, almost stubbornly, inept at images. If I understand how this particular lamp should look, it is only because, as a Chilean, I have seen countless replicas of it in my own country. In every beach house like this one, far away on that savage Pacific coast, lamps like this one await the night: except they display an added nuance of gray, are more banged up, more tired looking. The lamp that Roman is scrutinizing is a shade too bright, untinged, perhaps clean cut to a fault.

Roman Polanski by Susan Gray©

"The silver tint needs to be darkened," Roman declares finally. "It shouldn't shine like this."

He's right, of course. But how can he know? How can he possibly perceive something that subtle?

Polanski has never been to Chile, never stepped into the beach houses where I have spent months, never seen a photo of the sort of sad and tarnished lamp that occupies my mind. It is not research that gives him the right clues. He can, quite simply, grasp how the lamp should look, because for the last few months—and indeed for several years now—he has been imagining, object by object, board by board, the haunted and yet strangely ordinary place where Paulina will encounter and put on trial the man she thinks raped and tortured her fifteen years before. Now that the film is nearing the end of pre-production, he is taking his obsession with making everything coherent, inhabited, perfect, to unlikely extremes. Just to give one crazy example: Paulina's simulacrum of a kitchen is lined with closed cupboards. In them, filled to the brim, are mountains of authentic Chilean food staples in Chilean bags and tins imported specially from Santiago, halfway across the world. There is not one shot that calls for one of these cupboards to ever be opened, for the contents to be even remotely glimpsed through the shadows. But Roman needs them to be there, filling the corners of the unseen, lurking beyond the mere surface of perception, beyond what the camera captures, making the house breathe, secretly telling the characters where they are and who they have been and what they have eaten. It is this mania of Polanski's, the extended construction of a reliable imaginary, that warns him that the lamp with its healthy look would stand out, given all these other details, these billowing curtains, this light brown loaf of bread, these threatening knives, this sort of old-fashioned telephone, this Neruda woodcut, this stained table; that the lamp would call excessive attention to itself, would divert attention from what really matters: the madness and dissonances and troubles that are just underneath the surface of that world and that are about to explode. What really matters: human beings are trapped in that house with that lamp and with everything else in their lives, and we are going to watch them during the next few hours trying to escape from the tyranny of that reality, we are going to watch them try and bend that world to their desires, we are going to watch them succeed and we are going to watch them fail.

This is what Polanski does, has done, in film after stunning film: *Knife in the Water, Cul-de-Sac, Repulsion, Rosemary's Baby, Chinatown, Macbeth, Tess, The Tenant, Frantic, Bitter Moon.* Put us inside, deep inside the world he has created, on the frontier where illusion and pain meet, at times separate, and at times merge. And this is the paradox: Roman builds each space, each universe, to be as absolutely, incontrovertibly recognizable, unflinchingly familiar, horribly believable, so as to explore what is hidden, what is bizarre, what is absurd, so that the grid of reality can be tested against the inner demons of his characters, so that we can experience the liquid terror of being that person in that room, in that story, so that we can accompany that protagonist as he, as she, tries to change a destiny that has been imposed from somewhere else. Roman has spent his life mastering and using the techniques of realism in the service of the unspeakable.

So the lamp is there in order to help us understand what the lamp does not know, what cannot be seen immediately through

Roman has spent his life mastering and using the techniques of realism in the service of the unspeakable.

its glow: the almost inaccessible world of the mind and the heart, desperate for love, unable finally to touch other deeply enough to break out of solitude or delusion. And Polanski, once he has launched us on this voyage, will not relieve us with conclusive answers: his endings are almost invariably ambiguous, his heroes and heroines (if they may even be called by that name) haunted by the bite of uncertainty even as they dash their heads against the mirror of life. At times, as in *Repulsion* or *The Tenant*, they end up lost in insanity. But most of the time, as in *Knife in the Water* or *Tess* or *Death and the Maiden*, they end up lost in the bitter opposite of insanity: they end up lost in awareness, learning how vulnerable they are (they always were), how difficult it is to be moral, to be loved, in a world controlled by more powerful others. Donald Pleasance on his lonely rock in *Cul de Sac* and Mia Farrow alone with her devil's child in *Rosemary's Baby* or Jack Nicholson finally understanding who owns Los Angeles in *Chinatown*, all of them face-to-face with who they are, what the world is. The ferocious pull of Polanski's best films comes from his ability to implacably place us inside the impossible fantasies of his feverish protagonists and simultaneously force us to acknowledge them coldly, from afar, from the outside, from the history they cannot change. It is a vision Polanski rehearsed in his first short, *Two Men and a Wardrobe*, where the two Beckett-like fools emerge from the sea with their enormous wardrobe, are rejected by everyone as they wander the cruel city, and, unable to fit their oversized burden of the imagination anywhere, return to the waters and are swallowed by them.

Except that Roman was not swallowed. The waters did not close over him. In his art, he found the one possibility not open to his characters: a way of turning his vision away from the abyss of hallucination or the blind alley of frustration and into the shared and joyful realm of communal experience. This he has done at great personal expense, paying for the consequences of his independence, aggressively and often rambunctiously rejecting all compromises, refusing to apologize for the mystery of what he was seeing or the tangle of what he was communicating or the transgressions he lived, treading the dangerous line between the commercial and the artistic in a century that has not been kind to visionaries.

That is why Roman Polanski is the ultimate survivor: he has earned the right to inflict this vision on his spectators because he has always been willing to inflict it on himself.

Now, here, on the set of *Death and the Maiden*, he hands the lamp that is too pleasant and cheery to the prop master so that it can be darkened, so that it can help entice millions of eyes into his dreams, so that he can then close the door and not let those eyes out until they have caught a terrifying glimpse of what Roman's mind and life contain. He picks up some ropes. He looks at them for a while. He handles them. He ties them into a knot. He unties them. He makes a different knot. In a few more weeks, Sigourney Weaver will be using them to tie Ben Kingsley's hands. Are the ropes the right color? Are they too long? Are the edges too frayed? Would they be the sort a woman would have in her kitchen drawer at a beach house? He looks around at us. His eyes squint at me, at all of us. He is looking at me, but also through me, past me, somewhere else. He turns back to the ropes.

"There's something wrong," Roman says. "But you know, I can't figure out yet what it is, what's not right."

He will. He will.

FIRST WIFE

ANNE-MARIE LEVINE

He asked me so I said I would

He asked would I go through his dying with him

and I said yes, I said yes because what else could I say,

How could I say no

Afterwards I woke up crying every night

in the middle of the night and Bill,

Bill would hold me, wordlessly,

he never spoke there were never any words,

but I was crying for the parents,

I was imagining their grief and I took on their grief

and I thought I cried only for them

He asked would I go through it with him and I said yes

For me it was not so bad it was terrible

I lived through his death as my own so I knew

what it was I knew it long before it would happen

to me I was only forty   I figured now I knew

He called once would I come

and I went to the hospital and in the elevator

I met his wife and Why don't you go home she said

and I said I would go once he knew that I had come

When we met in his room he played us off

one against the other, not the least bit embarrassed

He was tickled silly to have us both there

When he died he was out of his mind, he was drugged

he was not unhappy   He was listening to Mozart,

the violin/piano sonatas played by Szymon Goldberg

and Lili Kraus, and he was pointing to a square of

paranoia on a spot opposite the bed, a spot where two walls met

It scared me to see him that way so I cried

but my crying scared the others so I left

If he had been clearheaded I could have stayed longer

He asked me to go there with him and I said yes

if he had been clearheaded I could have gone farther

I went as far as I could

GRANDMAMAN'S POKER DAY

COLETTE ROSSANT

In an excerpt from the upcoming 'Memories of a Lost Egypt; A Memoir with Recipes,' the noted French/Egyptian culinary writer recalls the monthly cooking chaos surrounding her grandmother's poker day.

My grandmother had many friends and relatives. Among her friends and family members were eight women who had known each other since they were children. A few, like Tante Marie, were widows with children; others had husbands who worked for my grandfather or were old friends of his. The eight spent hours on the telephone every day, exchanging gossip, talking about their children, or complaining about their servants, cooks, or daughters- and sons-in-law. Each woman had *son jour de recevoir*, her day to receive guests in the afternoon for a game of poker or canasta. Later, in early evening, their husbands would join them for dinner; after dinner, the women and the men would play high-stake games of poker until the wee hours of the morning. Hundreds and sometimes thousands of Egyptian pounds would pass hands, all in good fun.

I hated these days, since my life would be turned upside down. Grandmaman's day was Saturday, every eight weeks. Preparations started the day before. Early in the morning, before the sun got too hot, the whole household would be

· STUFFED GRAPE LEAVES ·

WASH A 1-POUND JAR OF VINE LEAVES under cold running water to rinse off the brine. Place in a bowl, cover with boiling water, and let stand for 5 minutes. Drain and cool.

MIX 1 POUND OF CHOPPED LAMB with 1 cup raw rice, $1/2$ cup chopped parsley, $1/3$ cup olive oil, $1/4$ cup lemon juice, 1 tablespoon cumin, and salt and pepper to taste. Mix well. Spread out the leaves. In the center of a vine leaf place 1 tablespoon of the meat-rice stuffing. Fold the base of the leaf up and over the stuffing, fold in the sides, and roll the leaf tightly to make a cylinder about $2 1/2$ inches long and $1/2$ to $3/4$ inch thick. Continue until you have used all the stuffing.

COVER THE BOTTOM of a heavy saucepan with loose vine leaves. Place a layer of stuffed vine leaves, close together and seam side down, along the bottom. Arrange another tightly packed layer on top of that, continuing until all the stuffed leaves have been added. Cover with 3 or 4 loose vine leaves. Pour in $1/4$ cup olive oil and 2 cups chicken broth. Cover and bring to a boil. Lower the heat and simmer for 45 minutes. When cooked, arrange the stuffed leaves on a platter and pour $1/4$ cup lemon juice over them. Serve hot or cold with yogurt or tehina. This makes about 30 to 40 vine leaves.

put to work cleaning the house, washing the terrace, and cooking a feast.

First the windows of the living room were flung wide open. Then the oriental rugs were picked up and tossed over the veranda railing. Abdullah would whip the dust off the rug with great energy, using a reed beater shaped like a four-leaf clover at the end of a long stick. While he beat, he sang a song. I would hear him and immediately appear in my nightgown and beg Abdullah to let me try. Within five minutes I would be covered with dust from head to toe. Suddenly my grandmother would appear, screaming at Abdullah that he had absolutely no brains allowing me do something so unladylike. She would grab me by the arm and banish me back to my rooms, ordering Aishe to give me a good scrubbing in the bathtub.

Afterward, the rugs would be put back in place, the furniture would be dusted, and four or five card tables would be set in the middle of the living room. Great quantities of flowers would arrive, and Marise, who was considered the artist of the family, would arrange them around the room. No one was allowed in the salon for the next twenty-four hours.

For poker day, the "good" silver, the most ornate and heavy cutlery, came out of the drawers, and the silver coffee service, which every Egyptian family seemed to have sitting on a silver tray on a sideboard, would be polished. Aishe and the porter's wife would be given the task of polishing the silver. I would sit with them, listening to their gossip about the men servants of the adjoining houses. Between polishing and gossiping they would munch on dried melon seeds, placing them between their front teeth and cracking them open. I learned very quickly how to do it, a habit to which my grandmother strongly objected. When they were afraid to eat the seeds because she was too near, they chewed on *mastic*, a sort of resin, transparent and hard as a stone, which would, after heroic chewing, turn into a sticky white paste.

When I was six, Aishe tried to teach me how to chew, but my baby teeth hurt so much that I quickly abandoned the idea, to the great relief of my grandmother, who loved to say about those who chewed, *"Ils ressemblent à des vaches espagnoles"* ("They look like Spanish cows"). I still don't chew gum and often try to stop my own grandchild Matthew from chewing bubble gum and blowing bubbles with it. Matthew thinks I am odd. "You're not an American, Grandmaman," he likes to say with a little smile as he tries to entice me to buy him some bubble gum.

On Fridays before poker days, Grandmaman and Ahmet would go together to the market, not in the open carriage, as when Grandmaman went to market with Abdullah, but in my grandfather's car. Ahmet sat next to the chauffeur, and I— when I was allowed to accompany them— would be in the backseat next to Grandmaman. On our return, my seat would filled with packages, and I would be squeezed in front between the chauffeur and Ahmet.

The scene at the market was quite different when Ahmet was with us. My grandmother was more subdued and would stand quietly to the side while Ahmet argued with the vendors about prices and quality of the food. However,

· APRICOT PUDDING ·

PLACE ½ POUND DRIED APRICOTS in a bowl. Cover with warm water and allow to soak overnight. Drain. Place the apricots, 4 large eggs, ¼ cup heavy cream, 1 tablespoon rum, and ½ cup sugar in a food processor. Process until the apricots are puréed. Butter a 1-quart mold. Pour the apricot purée into the mold. Place the mold in a larger pan filled with hot water and bake in a preheated 350-degree oven for 45 minutes, or until the point of a knife inserted in the middle comes out clean. Cool and unmold on a round platter. Garnish with mint leaves. This will serve 4.

one day a shattering event occurred; it might easily have destroyed my grandmother's favorite pastime had not Ahmet saved the day. We were standing between the poultry vendor and the watermelon vendor when suddenly Ahmet started to scream at a young man next to us, accusing him of stealing his money. A fight ensued, and suddenly it grew ugly. The crowd that gathered seemed hostile, and the man turned his attention to my grandmother and began hurling insults at her. I will never forget the fear on Grandmaman's face. She took me in her arms, enveloping me as if to protect me, nearly choking me while Ahmet and the watermelon man tried to calm the young man and the crowd. The police arrived, searched the young man, found Ahmet's wallet on him, and arrested him. They then escorted us back to the car. This was the only time I was allowed to sit in the back. My grandmother held me tightly, and I could feel her body still trembling from the fear that that incident had provoked. That night my grandfather scolded my grandmother and Ahmet and forbade Grandmaman ever to go shopping at the market again. For the next two months Grandmaman sent Ahmet to shop alone, but she missed the adventure of going to the market and soon resumed her weekly trips. I, however, had to wait a full year before I was allowed to accompany her.

With the poker-day cleaning and marketing done, the kitchen would be thrown into turmoil. Grandmaman herself would prepare her famous *sambusacks*, large eggplants would be charing on the primus, several legs of lamb would be marinating on the counter, and on a small table Aishe and the chauffeur would be stuffing grape leaves with a mixture of rice and chopped lamb. If I sat quietly near Aishe, I was allowed to stay in the kitchen and help roll the grape leaves. Meanwhile Ahmet would be preparing a ballottine of duck to be served sliced with a dark, smooth jelly. I loved to watch as Ahmet deftly cut the duck's back so it lay flat on the kitchen marble, then slowly and carefully deboned it. He would remove the duck meat, mince it with spices, and add pistachio nuts. The duck skin would then be rolled around the stuffing, and Ahmet with a needle and thread would sew it shut, making it look like a fat sausage. The scent of the roasting duck would permeate the house and make me very hungry. After a while, I would forget myself and begin chatting away, asking questions or begging a taste of something, often stealing some pistachios that Ahmet painstakingly had shelled that morning. Ahmet, in an unusual fit of exasperation, would then throw me out of the kitchen, and I would roam the house like a lost soul. I felt once more abandoned, for it seemed to me that I was nowhere welcomed.

My aunts prepared desserts. Tante

· STUFFED ZUCCHINI AND RED PEPPERS ·

HALVE ABOUT 1 POUND small zucchini and scoop out the centers. Cut the tops off 4 red bell peppers and remove all the seeds.

MIX 1 POUND CHOPPED BEEF with 1 pound chopped veal; add 3 tablespoons pine nuts, salt and pepper to taste, 2 minced garlic cloves, and 2 tablespoons olive oil. Fill the zucchini and the peppers with the meat. Place side by side in a pan. Drizzle with 2 tablespoons olive oil and add 2 cups chicken broth to the pan. Bake in a preheated 375-degree oven for 45 minutes. Serve hot or cold with yogurt. This is enough for 4.

• VEGETABLE SALAD •

PEEL, SEED, AND DICE 3 ripe tomatoes and 3 cucumbers. Dice 2 green bell peppers. Peel and chop 2 sweet white onions; chop 1 bunch parsley. Cube 2 red radishes, and peel and mince 2 garlic cloves. Dice 3 celery ribs and quarter 3 Bibb lettuces. Place all the vegetables in a large bowl. In a small bowl mix together 1 tablespoon Dijon mustard, 1 tablespoon red wine vinegar, 3 tablespoons olive oil, and salt and pepper to taste. Pour over the salad and toss. Serves 4.

served cold. *Hummus*, the traditional chickpea dish, was decorated with slivered almonds. There were also tiny artichoke hearts marinated in olive oil, fried ground chicken balls, and, in season, cold tender broad beans. Grandmaman's contribution to the *mezze* were "mimosa eggs," hard-boiled eggs stuffed with egg yolks mashed with mayonnaise and herbs, which I hated but which were very popular with the ladies. There were always thin slices of *batarekh*—salted dried roe of the gray mullet preserved in a sort of waxy skin—on thin toasts. Olives, black or green, would fill silver bowls, as would cucumber pickles. These dishes were served on the terrace while the table in the dining room was made ready for the dinner. Limoges dishes were brought out under the eyes of Grandmaman, who would repeat endlessly to everyone, "Be careful, be careful! These are my best dishes!"

Fortuné made her special dish of prunes stuffed with walnuts in a brandy syrup; Tante Lydia made a sort of multicolor tower of Jell-O that would invariably fall after the first person helped himself. It would look a mess, but Grandmaman never said anything because, as she explained to me one day, Lydia did not know how to cook. Tante Becca would bring a dish of her light, crisp, and golden *zalabia*, which I would gobble down if no one was looking.

Saturday morning, the remaining dishes were prepared. For the *mezze*, small pieces of lamb's liver were fried with onions and cumin; they would be sprinkled with lemon juice and minced parsley and

On this day the jewels came out, heavy

diamond-studded bracelets, arms full of gold bangles (by the age of ten, I had already ten of them), sparkling diamond rings. Grandmaman did not approve of diamonds and never wore hers. She would say of women covered in diamonds, "They look as if they are wearing a crystal chandelier!" I remember years later, when one of my uncles was trying to marry me off, he would always point out the quality of the pretenders by telling me how many karats my diamond would weigh.

My grandmother would tell me, just before the guests arrived, to go and get dressed, comb my hair, and, mainly, put some shoes on. Whenever I came back from school or was at home on weekends, I walked around the house barefoot or I wore shib-shib, the flat slippers that Aishe bought for me at the market. They made a flapping noise whenever I walked.

Sometimes a new person would be introduced to the group, and I would be proudly paraded in front of them. "My granddaughter," my grandmother would say to that day's new addition; "She is half French, you know," as if that qualification would add a new dimension to who I was. Then the whispers would start that always upset me: "She is an orphan, you know . . . Really? No, I did not know. . . . Well, not quite, her mother . . . you know . . . Alexandria . . . Beirut . . . left the child here with Marguerite . . ." And it would go on for several minutes. The women would look at me with pity, which I resented terribly, especially when my aunt Lydia would ask her younger daughter, Renée, who was just a year older than me, to come and say hello. Renée, tall, thin and blond, would gracefully make the rounds, and I would be forgotten as the women exclaimed in their chanting voices, "*Elle est adorable . . . comme elle est mignone!*" ("She is adorable . . . how pretty she is!").

The food was served twice on that day. When the ladies arrived around four o'clock, they would be served tea with petits fours from Groppi's, the famous

My grandfather had given her a strand of pearls for each of their nine children. It went several times around her neck, and while waiting her turn she would often play with the pearls, as if making a signal to her canasta partner.

• ANGEL HAIR WITH NUTS AND RAISINS •

BREAK ½ POUND of angel hair in 3-inch pieces. In a skillet heat 2 tablespoons butter with 1 tablespoon oil. Add 1 onion, thinly sliced; sauté until transparent. Add the angel hair and fry until golden brown. Cover with 3 cups chicken broth, bring to a boil, then lower the heat and simmer until all the broth is absorbed.

MEANWHILE ROAST 2 tablespoons slivered almonds and 2 tablespoons chopped hazelnuts in a 350-degree oven until golden. Remove from the oven. In a small skillet heat ½ tablespoon butter. Add 3 tablespoons raisins and sauté until the raisins puff up. Mix the raisins with nuts and add to the pasta. Serve hot with roast chicken. Serves 4.

Swiss pastry store in Cairo. Then they would sit around the four tables and begin to play. At each table was a member of the family. Grandmaman was always in a black lace blouse, and her pearls looked regal. She had told me the story of that pearl necklace: that my grandfather had given her a strand of pearls for each of their nine children. It went several times around her neck, and while waiting her turn she would often play with the pearls, as if making a signal to her canasta partner. "The pearls will be yours, Colette," she always said, "when you grow up and act like a real lady." Like Grandmaman, the others at the card table would also be all dressed up. Tante Fortuné was the one I admired the most. While everyone else was in black, her dresses would be of red silk covered with large blue roses, or of green velvet edged in gold. My grandmother was horrified. For her and her friends, once you got married you wore subdued colors, and by the time you were forty you wore black or gray. But Tante Fortuné would laugh and employ an argument that Grandmaman could never object to: "My husband loves it!" Years later at my own wedding, Tante Fortuné arrived in a black dress with an enormous red bow tied to her hips. The younger generation loved it, and she was the toast of the party.

While the women were playing, Renée and I were often asked to pass around little tea sandwiches, while Abdullah, dressed in his best *galabeyya*, would glide through the tables and ask which the women preferred, tea or coffee. The silver coffee set would be brought in, and European coffee, which was then very fashionable, would be served.

Within half an hour, though, we were forgotten. Renée would go back to her floor, and I would roam around the house, trying to find someone to talk to. Aishe was always too busy helping Ahmet; Ahmet would not allow me in the kitchen, and if I returned to the living room, my grandmother would signal me to get out and usually would say, "You are distracting the players!" I would end up in my room, sulking until dinner was announced.

Canasta was played with feverish intensity, and arguments sometimes broke out between partners over foolish melds or discards. Tante Marie's table was the most exciting. Tante Marie was an excellent player and often won the game. In the beginning, when my father and mother had settled in after we first came to Cairo, Tante Marie had tried to teach my mother how to play cards. Years later, when we were in Paris, my mother would tell me how much she hated cards, especially canasta, which she found very boring. Poker had seemed more exciting to her, but she had never learned it. She did try to learn bridge—a very popular game among the younger crowd—but even then, she wasn't very good at it. In defense of my mother, I too never learned how to play cards until years later, when I began to play games with my grandchildren. Julien, my youngest grandson, loves to play cards, and I can see in his eyes the same excitement and twinkle that Tante Marie had when she was winning.

Grandmaman always sat with her three best friends and, while playing, would continue to gossip. The women would finish the game, counting their winnings. My grandmother, who was not as good a player, did not often win.

Between seven and eight o'clock, the men would arrive and retire to the terrace, where Abdullah would serve the mezze. The women would join them there. This is when the younger members of the family—those not married—would arrive from the different floors of our house. My cousin Zaki called this moment the marriage-go-round. The unmarried young women of the family would slowly walk from table to table, greeting my grandmother's friends, talking about their projects, or simply smiling.

Later it would be the turn of the young unmarried men. The women would look over the young men for their daughters or the young women for their sons, mentally calculating the women's dowries, or the future earnings or fortunes of the men. Alice and Nadia, both in their late teens, would come down, parading among the guests, laughing and gossiping afterward, wondering aloud which one had made the best impression. Years later, Alice married an Englishman and moved to England, and Nadia moved to Italy and married an American who had settled there.

At eight-thirty, as dinner was announced, everyone, including the children, would move to the dining room to help themselves from the buffet while oohing and aahing about Ahmet's delicious cooking.

On the table for dinner would be the ballottine, beautifully decorated with egg white and jelly; roast leg of lamb, thinly sliced and served with a parsley sauce; hot, open meat pies with pine nuts; baked noodles with eggplant; several bowls of vegetable salads; cold fried fish served with *Zemino* sauce made with garlic and anchovies—one of my favorite dishes—and five different types of pickles. I would immediately pounce on the ballottine and the fried fish as my grandmother would shake her head in despair over my lack of manners.

Later, the women and men returned to the living room for serious games of poker, with much higher stakes. The names of the players were placed in a silver dish, then drawn to determine who would play with whom.

My grandfather always hoped to have Tante Marie at his table; just before picking up a name, he would make a small sign to my grandmother, trying to figure out which piece of paper bore Tante Marie's name.

Once everyone was sitting down and the card game had really begun, I was sent to bed. In the morning I would slide my hand under my pillow. If I found several pound notes, it meant that Tante Marie had won the night before. This was her gesture toward me, for she understood how lonely and forlorn I was on poker days.

The next morning, life's daily routine would return. The card tables were folded and put away, along with the Limoges china and the best silver. Ahmet would be in good humor, and I was allowed once again to haunt the kitchen when I came back from school, sample what was for dinner, and kick my shoes off.

TIN HOUSE:
THE NEXT TEN (OR SO) YEARS

GEORGE KALOGERAKIS

A very serious look at what is in store for Tin House.

➤ *Autumn 1999:* Second issue unsettles hard-core lit-mag buffs. The debut's all-around comprehensibility (*heuristic* and *mimetic* conspicuously absent from text; precious little discussion of *counter-hermeneutics*) and production values (horizontal-running type only; front of magazine clearly distinguishable from back) they had accepted as "ironic," but now they're starting to wonder.

➤ *Winter 1999:* Magazine continues to give rise to ferocious debate among connoisseurs of obscurantism. One morning, a brick crashes through office window with note reading "More language poetry" attached. While a minority still view the magazine's ongoing flirtation with competence as "defiantly dead-pan"—possibly even "cool"—there is a growing fear that, although a quarterly, *Tin House* might actually be readable.

➤ *Spring 2000:* That fear is put to rest with first theme issue, "The Lesser Poets of Latvia Reconsidered," which sells out.

➤ *Summer 2000:* Hitting their obtuse stride, editors intentionally print several pages out of sequence and, working closely with the art department, place random phrases upside-down (and, in one controversial instance, vertically and in a different font). Subscription renewals strong.

➤ *Winter 2000:* Critical success of Paul Theroux's essay "I Just Saw Naipaul Again and He Snubbed Me Again" is somewhat tempered by lawsuit from reader cut by errant staple protruding from binding.

➤ *Spring 2001:* "No staples were used in the creation of this magazine," reads the roof line: First perfect-bound issue-at 16 pages, the smallest the laws of physics will allow.

➢ *Autumn 2001*: "The Lumber Issue." Nod to quarterly's Northwest roots centers on 76-stanza epic poem based on Tennyson's "The Lady of Shalott," only it's about a chipmunk.

➢ *Summer 2002*: Having endlessly debated increasing size of magazine to either 8"x10" or 10"x15", editors impulsively re-design issue as stack of 3"x5" index cards (secured by a rubber band and assembled by hand), after the art department has gone home. She quits; a replacement is sought.

➢ *Winter 2002*: Rumors that Hachette is "interested in" *Tin House* traced to French-English paperback dictionary spotted among page proofs scattered on publisher's desk. Asked whether rumors are true, publisher offers a terse *"Non."*

➢ *Summer 2003*: The Supermodel really is dead, says *The New York Times*: Trend piece in business section notes *Tin House*'s shift away from abstract drawings of models on cover to abstract drawings of celebrities.

➢ *Autumn 2003*: Hachette rumor refuses to die. Cries of "sellout" are heard until magazine replaces contributors' bios with contributors' kindergarten report cards.

➢ *Winter 2003*: *Tin House* in the black. New office space! Still just four rooms, but now at least they're in two, not three different cities.

➢ *Spring 2004*: Fifth-anniversary issue. Updike on Wolfe; Wolfe on Updike; Mailer on Mailer.

➢ *Summer 2004*: *Tin House*'s belated on-line debut. Average time required to download issue—18 hours, owing to editors' belief that "we're a quarterly so this should take a while, anyway you've got three months to read it"—alienates some readers but delights print purists.

➢ *Autumn 2005*: "Egghead chic" sweeps Hollywood, again. Hot on the heels of Disney's seven-figure purchase of rights to *Academia Nuts!* (a teen comedy loosely based on office hijinx at *Lingua Franca*), Seagram's/DreamWorks options "Armenian Rhymed Couplets," which appears in a partial translation in this issue (the translator lost interest a third of the way through). Brad Pitt is already being talked about for lead gerund, pending revisions.

➢ *Spring 2006*: *Imponderables and Ponderables: A Tin House Reader* is published. Anthology greeted with tremendous acclaim ("B," *Entertainment Weekly* calls it, "-minus.")

➤ *Winter 2006*: Entire staff sacked after "the eggnog incident." Late during closing party, an unstable contributor silences the room by claiming to have once been paid by the magazine; melee ensues. Everyone is rehired after the contributor disavows offending statement ("it was the nutmeg talking") and promises to seek help.

➤ *Summer 2007*: "Summer Fun" issue. Magazine given over completely to 15,000-word David Foster Wallace footnote, with readers invited to mail in postcard to receive rest of manuscript. (Nominated for National Magazine Award in "Single-Theme Issue" category for publications with a circulation under 500.)

➤ *Winter 2007*: *Tin House* paralyzed by pitched battle between East and West Coast staffs. Portland office has lovingly prepared "Winter = Death" cover; New York office prefers "Portland = Death." Publisher's garbled order to "um, split the, um, run" (go half-and-half) is misunderstood by intern. Resulting cover—"Death = Death"—is lowest seller ever. (The few "Portland = Winter" copies that inexplicably trickle out are warmly received.)

➤ *Spring 2008*: Attempting to "recapture the magic," *Tin House* emergency-airlifts newly reconsidered lesser Latvian poets to Planet Hollywood parties in New York and Portland. Euphoria dampened by brawl between newly reconsidered lesser Latvian poets and chronically unconsidered Southwest story writers.

➤ *Autumn 2008*: Rumors that Condé Nast is "interested in" *Tin House* traced to Prada bag spotted among page proofs scattered on publisher's desk. Other, entirely unrelated rumors, traced to same Prada bag.

➤ *Spring 2009*: Tenth-anniversary issue. Ellis on McInerney; McInerney on Ellis; Mailer on Mailer.

➤ *Autumn 2009*: *Tin House* purchased by Condé Nast Publications. Condé Nast Editorial Director Mark Golin (ex-*Maxim*, -*Details*, -*GQ*, -*New Yorker*, -*Golin's Content*) pledges no interference.

➤ *Winter 2009*: *Tin House*—now renamed *New House* (after brief flirtations with *TH*, *Florio's*, and *Bazongas*)—moves into portion of 4 Times Square office suite left vacant by the *Bride's*-*Vanity Fair* merger. Work begins on "Binky's Beach Blanket Bingo," raunchy swimsuit issue featuring literary agents cavorting with their pet first-novelists. 🏠

CROSSWORD

ANAGRAMMED AUTHORS

EMILY COX AND HENRY RATHVON

ACROSS

1 Dramatist whose name anagrams into "mad phrases" (2 wds.: 3,7)

6 Character in many Updike stories

10 Writer whose name has a Ring to it

11 With 18 Across, children's author whose anagram is "a nice dark muse" (2 wds.: 7,6)

12 Poet whose anagram is "delve into verse" (2 wds.: 6,8)

13 Shortened, as a dictionary

15 Home of some ancient Greek tragedians

18 See 11 Across

20 Board game for word lovers

23 Poet whose anagram is "I'm docile, skinny" (2 wds.: 5,9)

26 Quiddity, or inmost nature

27 Caldwell the novelist

28 What Prince Charming used to wake Sleeping Beauty

29 Author who produces "humane work," anagrammatically (2 wds.: 6,4)

DOWN

1 The Bard's term for youth in Antony and Cleopatra (2 wds.: 5,4)

2 Narrator in a Coleridge poem

3 What Pilate washed symbolically

4 Like lines that never touch

5 Extract

7 Installment of a serialized story

8   David Copperfield villain Uriah

9   Legendary Roman matron violated by Sextus

14   What might loom for a procrastinating writer

16   Author of Cannery Row

17   Wallace Stevens poem "The Emperor of ___" (2 wds.: 3,5)

19   Goddess of vengeance, or downfall

21   Code of ethics for samurai warriors

22   Stick fast, like tape

24   The Master Builder playwright

25   Actor who portrayed a Harper Lee hero

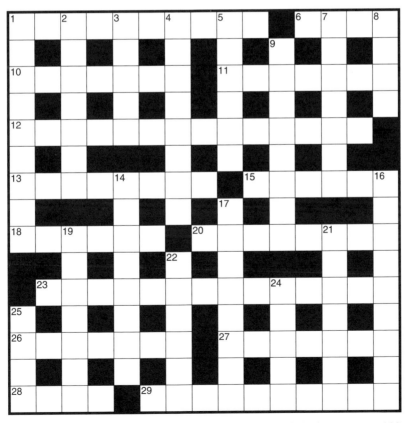

Solution on page 183

CONTRIBUTORS

AGHA SHAHID ALI'S poetry collections include *The Half-Inch Himalayas, A Walk Through the Yellow Pages, A Nostalgist's Map of America, The Belovéd Witness: Selected Poems*, and—most recently, *The Country Without a Post Office* (W. W. Norton), a collection that focuses on the current turmoil in Kashmir, where he is from. He is also the translator of *The Rebel's Silhouette: Selected Poems by Faiz Ahmed Faiz*, as well as the author of *T.S. Eliot as Editor*. He is on the poetry faculty of the M.F.A. Creative Writing Program at the University of Massachusetts, Amherst, and is currently a visiting professor at Princeton University.

NUAR ALSADIR lives in New York City.

RON CARLSON is the author of five books of fiction; the story collections *The Hotel Eden* (which was selected as one of the notable books of 1997 by The New York Times and one of the top 100 books of the year by The L.A. Times), *Plan B for the Middle Class* and *The News of the World*; and two novels, *Truants*, and *Betrayed by Scott Fitzgerald*. His fiction has appeared in *Harper's, Gentlemen's Quarterly, Esquire, Witness*, and other journals and anthologies, including *The Norton Anthology of Short Fiction, The Best American Short Stories*, and *Sudden Fiction*. Mr. Carlson has been awarded a National Endowment for the Arts Fellowship in Fiction, a Pushcart Prize, and the Ploughshares Cohen Prize. He is Professor of English at Arizona State University and lives with Elaine Carlson and their two sons in Scottsdale, Arizona.

CHRISTINA CHIU is a co-founder of the Asian American Writers' Workshop. A recipient of the Van Lier Fellowship, she is completing her M.F.A. at Columbia University.

EMILY COX and HENRY RATHVON began creating puzzles professionally in the 1970s. Their puzzles regularly appear in *The Atlantic Monthly, The Boston Globe, The New Yorker, The Wall Street Journal*, Canada's *National Post*, and other publications. On the World Wide Web, they monitor a crossword chat forum for *The New York Times*. They live in Hershey, Pennsylvania with a full-size skeleton of the quintessential crossword bird, the emu.

ALEŠ DEBELJAK is chair of the Cultural Studies department at the University of Ljubljana, Slovenia. He has published five collections of poems, six books of cultural criticism, and a translation of John Ashbery's poetry into his native Slovenian. He was a fellow at the

Collegium Budapest-Institute for Advanced Study and a senior Fulbright fellow at the University of California, Berkeley. He has won several awards for his creative work, including the Slovenia National Book Award and Miriam Lindberg Israel Poetry for Peace Prize (Tel Aviv).

ARIEL DORFMAN is the author of numerous novels, plays and books of non-fiction, including *Hard Rain*; *Konfidenz*, and *How to Read Donald Duck* (with Armand Mattelart). His work has been translated into thirty languages. His latest work includes a memoir, *Heading South, Looking North: A Bilingual Journey*, published by Farrar Strauss in 1998, and the novel *The Nanny and the Iceberg*, forthcoming in Spring, 1999. He also has written and produced several films. His essay on Roman Polanski will be included in the anthology, *Writers on Directors*, featuring photographs of Susan Gray, and published by Watson-Guptill Publications.

STUART DYBEK is the author of the story collections *The Coast of Chicago* and *Childhood and Other Neighborhoods*. His poems have appeared in *Poetry,*

The Gettysburg Review, and *Triquarterly*. A novella of his was recently published in *DoubleTake*. He lives in Kalamazoo, Michigan.

PHILIP FRIED is a New York-based poet and little-magazine editor. He is the author of two books of poetry, *Mutual Trespasses* and *Quantum Genesis* and is currently completing a third volume. He recently collaborated with his wife, the photographer Lynn Saville, on a book that combines her nocturnal photographs with night-inspired poetry from around the world, *Acquainted with the Night*. He is the founder of *The Manhattan Review*.

ALBERTO FUGUET is the author of a collection of short stories, *Be Kind, Rewind (Por Favor, Robobinar)*, and three novels, *Overdose, Tinta Roja*, and *Bad Vibes (Mala Ondo)*, which was translated into English in 1998. He has edited an anthology of new South American writers called *McOndo* and is currently on a Fullbright scholarship at Georgetown University.

ANGELICA VANESSA GARNETT, born in 1918, is the daughter of Vanessa Bell, Virginia Woolf's sister, and Duncan Grant, central figures in Bloomsbury. Brought up to think of herself as Clive Bell's daughter, Angelica was only told of the identity of her true father at the age of seventeen. She grew up in London and Sussex, and married David Garnett in 1942 with whom she had four daughters. Her memoir, *Deceived with Kindness*, was published in 1984. She lives in France.

DAVID GATES is the author of two novels, *Jernigan* and *Preston Falls*, which was recently nominated for the National Book Critics Circle Award. A collection of stories, *The Wonders of the Invisible World*, will be published in June, 1999 by Knopf.

JOANNA GOODMAN lives and teaches in New York City. Her poetry and translations have appeared, or will soon appear, in *Massachusetts Review, Seneca Review, Sonora Review, Denver Quarterly, Phoebe, Indiana Review, World Literature Today, Fence, Modern Poetry In Translation* and *The Literary Review*, which will run a feature of her work in its Fall '99 issue. She is currently completing her first poetry manuscript, titled *False Alarm*. A short quote from Wallace Stevens' *Meditation Celestial & Terrestrial* has been incorporated into "Coming of Age."

FRAN GORDON directs the National Arts Club PAGE reading series. She is currently working on a nonfiction book about 21st Century writers. Her first novel, *Paisley Girl*, is forthcoming from St. Martins in Fall, 1999.

MICHAEL HAINEY was born in Chicago and now lives in Manhattan. "Autumn Comes to Chicago" is his first published poem.

RACHEL KADISH is the author of the novel *From a Sealed Room*. She was a fiction fellow at Radcliffe's Bunting Institute. She lives in Cambridge, Massachusetts.

GEORGE KALOGERAKIS is an editor at *New York Magazine*. He has also worked as a writer and editor for *Vogue, Vanity Fair,* and *Spy*.

JAMES KELMAN'S novels include *A Chancer, A Disaffection* and *How late it was, how late*. His story collections include *Greyhound for Breakfast* and *Busted Scotch*. He lives in Glasgow, but is spending the 1998-1999 academic year as a writer in residence at the University of Texas in Ausin. "Yeh, these stages" was first published in Great Britain in 1998 by Secker & Warburg, and is included in his forthcoming collection, *The Good Times*, which will be published by Doubleday in June, 1999.

ANNE-MARIE LEVINE'S book of poems, *EUPHORBIA* was chosen as a finalist in the Paterson Poetry Prize 1995. Her poetry has appeared in *Salamander, Provincetown Arts*, and *Parnassus*. Winner of a fellowship in poetry from the New York Foundation for the Arts, she is the founder of *Poets & Performers* and is on the Board of Directors of Poets House in New York.

JIM LEWIS is the author of the novels *Sister* and *Why the Tree Loves the Ax*.

RICHARD MCCANN is the author of *Ghost Letters* (1994 Beatrice Hawley Award, 1994 Capricorn Poetry Award) and editor (with Michael Klein) of *Things Shaped in Passing: More 'Poets for Life' Writing from the AIDS Pandemic*. His fiction and poetry have appeared in *The Atlantic, Esquire, The Nation*, and *Ploughshares*, and in numerous anthologies. He co-directs the graduate program in creative writing at American University in Washington, D.C.

CHRISTOPHER MERRILL'S books include *Watch Fire* (poetry), *The Old*

Bridge: The Third Balkan War and the Age of the Refugee (nonfiction), and the translation of Aleš Debeljak's *Anxious Moments*. He holds the William H. Jenks Chair in Contemporary Letters at the College of the Holy Cross.

RICK MOODY is the author of the novels *The Ice Storm* and *Purple America*, and a collection of stories, *The Ring of Brightest Angels Around Heaven*.

PIPO is a photographer living in San Francisco. His work is published courtesy of The Elizabeth Leach Gallery in Portland, Oregon.

COLLETTE ROSSANT is a columnist for *The New York Daily News* and a contributor to many food and travel magazines. She is the author of eight cookbooks and lives in New York City. "Gramaman's Poker Day" is excerpted from *Memoirs of a Lost Egypt*; a memoir with recipes, to be published April, 1999 by Clarkson Potter.

RACHEL RESNICK'S first novel, *Go West, Young F*cked Up Chick*, will be published in April, 1999 by St. Martins Press. She lives in Topanga, California.

FRANCINE PROSE'S most recent book is the novella collection *Guided Tours of Hell*. She is the author of ten novels, including *Hunters and Gatherers, Primitive People*, and *Household Saints*. She is a regular contributor to *The New York Times, The New York Observer* and *Newsday*. The recipient of numerous grants and awards, Prose teaches at the New School and the Sewanee Writer's Conference.

HELEN SCHULMAN is the author of the novels *The Revisionist* and *Out of Time*, and a collection of stories, *Not A Free Show*. She is also a co-editor, along with Jill Bialosky, of an anthology of essays, *Wanting A Child*. Her stories, essays and reviews have appeared in *Time, Vanity Fair, Vogue, Gentlemen's Quarterly, The Paris Review, Story*, and *Ploughshares*, among other publications. She presently teaches in the Graduate Writing Division of Columbia University.

CHARLES SIMIC'S first full-length collection of poems, *What the Grass Says*, was published in 1967. Since then, he has published more than sixty books in the U.S. and abroad, including *Jackstraws* (forthcoming in Spring, 1999 from Harcourt Brace); *Walking the*

Black Cat, which was a finalist for the National Book Award in poetry; *A Wedding in Hell*; *Hotel Insomnia*; *The World Doesn't End: Prose Poems*, for which he received a Pulitzer Prize for Poetry; *Selected Poems: 1963-83*; and *Unending Blues*. He also has published many translations of French, Serbian, Croatian, Macedonian, and Slovenian poetry, and four books of essays, most recently *Orphan Factory*. His many awards include fellowships from the Guggenheim Foundation, the MacArthur Foundation, and the National Endowment for the Arts. He is Professor of English at the University of New Hampshire.

DAVID FOSTER WALLACE is the author of a collection of essays, *A Supposedly Fun Thing I'll Never Do Again,* the novels *Infinite Jest* and *The Broom of the System*, as well as the short story collection, *Girl with Curious Hair*. A recipient of a MacArthur Foundation award, his writing has appeared in *The Paris Review* and *Harper's*, among other publications. "On His Deathbed, Holding Your Hand, the Acclaimed New Young Off-Broadway Play-wright's Father Begs a Boon" will

appear in the collection *Brief Interviews with Hideous Men*, from Little, Brown, in May, 1999.

C.K. WILLIAMS' most recent poetry collections include *Selected Poems* and *The Vigil*. He is the recipient of a PEN/Voelcker Award, A National Book Critics Circle Award nomination, a Pulitzer Prize nomination, and the Berlin Prize. "Tender" and "The Poet" will be included in his collection *Repair*, from Farrar, Straus, Giroux, in June, 1999.

Crossword Solution

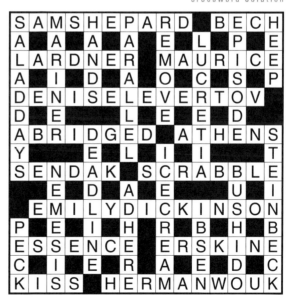

IN GRAVITY NATIONAL PARK

Poems

C. L. Rawlins

"Rawlins is that rare being: *a whole man*, a compassionate philosopher, and an artist of the written word (see his astonishing double sestina about life underground in a working mine.). Be sure to explore *In Gravity National Park*. You'll want to return to it again and again."

—Carolyn Kizer

80 pages, paperback, 0-87417-322-1, $11.00
Western Literature Series

BATHING IN THE RIVER OF ASHES

Poems

Shaun Griffin

"The force of sympathy in these poems is so great that it virtually runs off the page, like sweat or blood. They are compelling poems, not solely because of their expressive feeling but because of their honesty and their unflinching vision of what is."—Hayden Carruth

72 pages, paperback, 0-87417-331-0, $11.00
Western Literature Series

THE HOUSE ON BREAKAHEART ROAD

Poems

Gailmarie Pahmeier

"Pahmeier's is a purely American poetry, a tough female vision that includes the language of baseball and bread baking, well-tuned transmissions and hard-packed snow, truckstops and 'wound-red lipstick.'"—Dorianne Laux

72 pages, paperback, 0-87417-313-2, $10.00
Western Literature Series

▲▲UNIVERSITY OF NEVADA PRESS
CALL TOLL FREE TO ORDER: 1-877-NVBOOKS
Mail Stop 166 • Reno, NV 89557-0076 • phone (775) 784-6573 • fax (775) 784-6200

LITERARY ARTS

Oregon Book Awards

Oregon Literary Fellowships

Portland Arts & Lectures

Poetry in Motion™

Writers in the Schools

Celebrating and Encouraging
the Power and Impact of the
Written Word

720 SW Washington, Suite 700
Portland, OR 97205
tel 503/227-2583   fax 503/241-7429
email la@literary-arts.org
web www.literary-arts.org

Established in 1986, the Laura Russo Gallery is one of the most beautiful showcases for art in the Pacific Northwest, exhibiting some of the highest quality arworkt available. We represent contemporary Northwest artists working in a variety of media including paintings, sculpture, works on paper, and fine art prints, in a diversity of styles, from landscape to abstract expressionism.

May
    Otto Fried - Paintings
    and Sculpture
    Rae Mahafffey -
    Domestic Scenes,
    Paintings and Prints
June
    Angelita Surmon -
    Recent Paintings
    Works on Paper by
    gallery artists
July
    Sean Cain - Paintings
    New Views

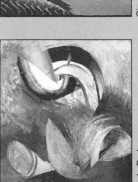

Cie Goulet

Lucinda Parker

Gregory Grenon

Representing the finest in Contemporary Northwest Art.

Artists include:

Jay Backstrand	Dana Lynn Louis
Marlene Bauer	Rae Mahaffey
Frank Boyden	Alden Mason
Michael Brophy	Stephen McClelland
Robert Colescott	Nancy Mee
Michael Dailey	William Moore
Dennis Evans	Lucinda Parker
Judith P. Fawkes	Jack Portland
Tom Fawkes	René Rickabaugh
Chris Gander	Michele Russo
Cie Goulet	Angelita Surmon
Paul Green	Margot Thompson
Gregory Grenon	Gina Wilson
Sally Haley	and others
Frederick Heidel	
Manuel Izquierdo	and the Estates of:
Fay Jones	Louis Bunce
Mary Josephson	Kenneth Callahan
Mel Katz	Carl Morris
Michihiro Kosuge	Hilda Morris

Enjoy the Benefit of Saving 50% Off the Cover Price of *Tin House* When You Become a Charter Subscriber

· · · · · ·

SIMPLY FILL OUT AND SEND THE CARD BELOW (THE POSTAGE IS FREE) TO BEGIN
RECEIVING 'TIN HOUSE' FOR ONLY $19.95!

50% OFF

COVER

PRICE

· · · · ·

THE

LITERARY

MAGAZINE

PEOPLE

ACTUALLY

WANT TO

READ

☑ YES! I want to become a charter subscriber and begin receiving *Tin House*. Please enter my charter subscription and bill me next month. I'll receive the next four issues (one year's worth) for only $19.95, saving me half off the cover price!

NAME ....

ADDRESS ....

CITY .... STATE .... ZIP ....

☐ BILL ME NEXT MONTH   ☐ PAYMENT ENCLOSED   PREM01

☑ YES! I want to become a charter subscriber and begin receiving *Tin House*. Please enter my charter subscription and bill me next month. I'll receive the next four issues (one year's worth) for only $19.95, saving me half off the cover price!

NAME ....

ADDRESS ....

CITY .... STATE .... ZIP ....

☐ BILL ME NEXT MONTH   ☐ PAYMENT ENCLOSED   PREM01

BUSINESS REPLY MAIL
FIRST-CLASS MAIL PERMIT NO 1158 PORTLAND OR

POSTAGE WILL BE PAID BY ADDRESSEE

NO POSTAGE
NECESSARY
IF MAILED
IN THE
UNITED STATES

TIN HOUSE
PO BOX 10500
PORTLAND OR 97296-9924

BUSINESS REPLY MAIL
FIRST-CLASS MAIL PERMIT NO 1158 PORTLAND OR

POSTAGE WILL BE PAID BY ADDRESSEE

NO POSTAGE
NECESSARY
IF MAILED
IN THE
UNITED STATES

TIN HOUSE
PO BOX 10500
PORTLAND OR 97296-9924